Erle Stanley Gardner and The Murder Room

>>> This title is part of The Murder Room, our series dedicated to making available out-of-print or hard-to-find titles by classic crime writers.

Crime fiction has always held up a mirror to society. The Victorians were fascinated by sensational murder and the emerging science of detection; now we are obsessed with the forensic detail of violent death. And no other genre has so captivated and enthralled readers.

Vast troves of classic crime writing have for a long time been unavailable to all but the most dedicated frequenters of second-hand bookshops. The advent of digital publishing means that we are now able to bring you the backlists of a huge range of titles by classic and contemporary crime writers, some of which have been out of print for decades.

From the genteel amateur private eyes of the Golden Age and the femmes fatales of pulp fiction, to the morally ambiguous hard-boiled detectives of mid twentieth-century America and their descendants who walk our twenty-first century streets, The Murder Room has it all. >>>

The Murder Room
Where Criminal Minds Meet

themurderroom.com

Erle Stanley Gardner (1889–1970)

Born in Malden, Massachusetts, Erle Stanley Gardner left school in 1909 and attended Valparaiso University School of Law in Indiana for just one month before he was suspended for focusing more on his hobby of boxing that his academic studies. Soon after, he settled in California, where he taught himself the law and passed the state bar exam in 1911. The practise of law never held much interest for him, however, apart from as it pertained to trial strategy, and in his spare time he began to write for the pulp magazines that gave Dashiell Hammett and Raymond Chandler their start. Not long after the publication of his first novel, *The Case of the Velvet Claws*, featuring Perry Mason, he gave up his legal practice to write full time. He had one daughter, Grace, with his first wife, Natalie, from whom he later separated. In 1968 Gardner married his long-term secretary, Agnes Jean Bethell, whom he professed to be the real 'Della Street', Perry Mason's sole (although unacknowledged) love interest. He was one of the most successful authors of all time and at the time of his death, in Temecula, California in 1970, is said to have had 135 million copies of his books in print in America alone.

By Erle Stanley Gardner
(titles below include only those
published in the Murder Room)

Perry Mason series

The Case of the Sulky Girl
(1933)
The Case of the Baited Hook
(1940)
The Case of the Borrowed
Brunette (1946)
The Case of the Lonely
Heiress (1948)
The Case of the Negligent
Nymph (1950)
The Case of the Moth-Eaten
Mink (1952)
The Case of the Glamorous
Ghost (1955)
The Case of the Terrified
Typist (1956)
The Case of the Gilded Lily
(1956)
The Case of the Lucky Loser
(1957)
The Case of the Long-Legged
Models (1958)
The Case of the Deadly Toy
(1959)
The Case of the Singing Skirt
(1959)

The Case of the Duplicate
Daughter (1960)
The Case of the Blonde
Bonanza (1962)

Cool and Lam series

The Bigger They Come (1939)
Turn on the Heat (1940)
Gold Comes in Bricks (1940)
Spill the Jackpot (1941)
Double or Quits (1941)
Owls Don't Blink (1942)
Bats Fly at Dusk (1942)
Cats Prowl at Night (1943)
Crows Can't Count (1946)
Fools Die on Friday (1947)
Bedrooms Have Windows
(1949)
Some Women Won't Wait (1953)
Beware the Curves (1956)
You Can Die Laughing (1957)
Some Slips Don't Show (1957)
The Count of Nine (1958)
Pass the Gravy (1959)
Kept Women Can't Quit (1960)
Bachelors Get Lonely (1961)
Shills Can't Count Chips (1961)

Try Anything Once (1962)
Fish or Cut Bait (1963)
Up For Grabs (1964)
Cut Thin to Win (1965)
Widows Wear Weeds (1966)
Traps Need Fresh Bait (1967)

Doug Selby D.A. series

The D.A. Calls it Murder (1937)
The D.A. Holds a Candle (1938)
The D.A. Draws a Circle (1939)
The D.A. Goes to Trial (1940)
The D.A. Cooks a Goose (1942)
The D.A. Calls a Turn (1944)
The D.A. Takes a Chance (1946)
The D.A. Breaks an Egg (1949)

Terry Clane series

Murder Up My Sleeve (1937)
The Case of the Backward
  Mule (1946)

Gramp Wiggins series

The Case of the Turning Tide
  (1941)
The Case of the Smoking
  Chimney (1943)

Two Clues (two novellas) (1947)

Bats Fly at Dusk

Erle Stanley Gardner

An Orion book

Copyright © The Erle Stanley Gardner Trust 1942

The right of Erle Stanley Gardner to be identified as the author of this work has been asserted in accordance with the Copyright, Designs and Patents Act 1988.

This edition published by
The Orion Publishing Group Ltd
Orion House
5 Upper St Martin's Lane
London WC2H 9EA

An Hachette UK company
A CIP catalogue record for this book is available from the British Library

ISBN 978 1 4719 0888 0

www.orionbooks.co.uk

Chapter One

THE SIGN on the door said *Cool & Lam, Confidential Investigations*. But the blind man couldn't see the sign. The elevator starter had given him the room number, and the tapping cane, starting with the first door at the corner of the corridor, had patiently counted the doors until the frail, bony silhouette was etched in black against the frosted glass of the entrance office.

Elsie Brand looked up from her typewriting, saw the thin old man, the heavy, dark glasses, the striped cane, and the tray with the neckties, the lead pencils, and the tin cup. Her fingers ceased pounding the keyboard.

The blind man spoke before she had a chance to say anything.

"Mrs. Cool."

"Busy."

"I'll wait."

"It won't do any good."

For a moment, the man seemed puzzled; then a wan smile tugged at the hollowed cheeks. "It's about business," he said and, after a half second, added, "I have money."

Elsie Brand said, "That's different." She reached for the telephone, thought better of it, kicked her chair back from the typewriter desk, swiveled around, said, "Wait a minute," and crossed the office to open the door marked: *B. Cool, Private*.

Bertha Cool, somewhere in the fifties, a hundred and sixty-five pounds of cold realism, sat in the big swivel chair at the desk and regarded Elsie Brand with gray-eyed skepticism.

1

"Well, what is it?"

"A blind man."

"Young or old?"

"Old. A street vendor with a tray of neckties, a tin cup, and—"

"Throw him out."

"He wants to see you—on business."

"Any money?"

"He says he has."

"What sort of business?"

"He didn't say."

Bertha's eyes glittered at Elsie Brand. "Show him in. What the hell are you standing there for? If he's got business and he has money, what more do we want?"

Elsie said, "I just wanted to make certain," and opened the door. "Come in," she said to the blind man.

The cane tapped its way across the office, entered Bertha's inner sanctum. Once inside the room, the man paused inquiringly, holding his head cocked slightly on one side, listening intently.

His keen ears caught the sound of some slight motion Bertha made. He turned toward her as though he could see her, bowed, and said, "Good morning, Mrs. Cool."

"Sit down," Bertha said. "Elsie, get that chair out for him. That's fine. That's all, Elsie. Sit down, Mr.—What's your name?"

"Kosling. Rodney Kosling."

"All right, sit down. I'm Bertha Cool."

"Yes, I know. Where is the young man who works with you, Mrs. Cool? Donald Lam, I believe his name is."

Bertha's face became grimly savage. "Damn him!" she sputtered.

"Where is he?"

"In the Navy."

"Oh."

"He enlisted," Bertha said. "I had things fixed so he was deferred—took a war contract just to have something that would beat the draft. Worked things slick as a whistle; got him classified as an indispensable worker in an essential industry—and then the damn little runt goes and enlists in the Navy."

"I miss him," Kosling said simply.

Bertha frowned at him. "*You* miss him? I didn't know that you knew him."

He smiled slightly. "I think I know every one of the regulars."

"What do you mean?"

"My station is down half a block in front of the bank building on the corner."

"That's right. Come to think of it, I've seen you there."

"I know almost everyone that passes."

"Oh," Bertha said, "*I* see," and laughed.

"No, no," he corrected her hastily. "It isn't that. I really *am* blind. It's the steps I can tell."

"You mean you can recognize the steps of different people out of a whole crowd?"

"Of course," Kosling said simply. "People walk as distinctively as they do anything else. The length of steps. the rapidity of the steps, the little dragging of the heels, the— Oh, there are a dozen things. And then, of course, I occasionally hear their voices. Voices help a lot. You and Mr. Lam, for instance, were nearly always talking as you walked past. That is, *you* were. You were asking him questions about the cases he was working on when you'd go to work in the morning, and at night you'd be urging him to speed things up and get results for the clients. He rarely said much."

"He didn't need to," Bertha grunted. "Brainiest little cuss I ever got hold of—but erratic. Going out and joining the Navy shows the crazy streak in him. All settled down with a deferred rating, making good money, just recently taken into the business as a full partner—and he goes and joins the Navy."

"He felt his country needed him."

Bertha said grimly, "And *I* feel that *I* need him."

"I always liked him," the blind man said. "He was thoughtful and considerate. Guess he was pretty well up against it when he started with you, wasn't he?"

"He was so hungry," Bertha said, "his belt buckle was cutting his initials in his backbone. I took him in, gave him a chance to earn a decent living; then he worked his way into the partnership, and then—and then he goes away and leaves me flat."

Kosling's voice was reminiscent. "Even when he was pretty well down on his luck, he'd always have a pleasant word for me. Then when he began to get a little money, he started dropping coins—but he never dropped coins when you were with him. When he dropped money, he wouldn't speak to me." The blind man smiled reminiscently, and then went on. "As though I didn't know who he was. I knew his step as well as I knew his voice, but he thought it would embarrass me less if I didn't know who was making the donation—as though a beggar had any pride left. When a man starts begging, he takes money from anyone who will give it to him."

Bertha Cool straightened up behind the desk. "All right," she said crisply. "Speaking of money, what do you want?"

"I want you to find a girl."

"Who is she?"

"I don't know her name."

"What does she look like? Oh, I'm sorry."

"It's all right," the blind man said. "Here's all I know about her. She works within a radius of three blocks from here. It's a well-paid job. She's about twenty-five or twenty-six. She's slender, weighs about a hundred and six or a hundred and seven pounds, and is about five feet four inches tall."

"How do you know all that?" Bertha asked.

"My ears tell me."

"Your ears don't tell you where she works," Bertha said.

"Oh, yes, they do."

"I'll bite," Bertha said. "What's the gag?"

"No gag. I always know what time it is on the hour. There's a clock that chimes the hours."

"What's that got to do with it?"

"She'd walk past me anywhere from five minutes of nine to about three minutes of nine. When she walked by about three minutes of nine, she'd be walking fast. At five minutes to nine, she'd be walking more slowly. The jobs that start at nine o'clock are the better class of jobs. Most stenographic jobs in the district start at eight-thirty. I can tell about how old she is from her voice; how tall she is from the length of her steps; and what she weighs from the sound of her feet on the sidewalk. You'd be surprised at what your ears will tell you when you really learn to rely on them."

Bertha Cool thought that over for a moment, then said, "Yes, I guess so."

"When you go blind," Kosling explained, "you either feel that you're shut away from the world, can't take part in life, and lose interest in it; or you keep an interest in life, and decide you're going to get along with what you have, and make the best of it. You've probably noticed that people know a lot about the things they're interested in."

Bertha Cool detoured the opportunity to discuss philosophy and brought the subject back to dollars and cents. "Why do you want me to find this girl? Why can't you find her yourself?"

"She was hurt in an automobile accident at the street intersection. It was about a quarter to six in the evening, last Friday. She'd been working late at the office, I think, and was hurrying as she walked past me. Perhaps she had a date and was in a hurry to get home and get her clothes changed. I don't think she'd taken over two steps off the curb when I heard the scream of tires, a thud, and then the girl cried out in pain. I heard people running. A man's voice asked her if she was hurt, and she laughed and said no; but she was badly scared and shaken up. He insisted that she go to a hospital for a checkup. She refused. Finally she said she'd let him give her a lift. When she was getting in the car, she said her head hurt and that perhaps it would be well to be examined by a doctor. She didn't come back Saturday, and she wasn't back

Monday. This is Tuesday, and she isn't back today. I want you to find her."

"What's *your* interest in her?" Bertha asked.

The blind man's smile was benign. "You may put it down as a charitable impulse," he said. "I make my living out of charity, and—well, perhaps this girl needs help."

Bertha stared coldly at him. "I don't make *my* living out of charity. It's going to cost you ten dollars a day and a minimum of twenty-five dollars. If we don't have any results when the twenty-five dollars is used up, you can decide whether you want to go ahead at ten dollars a day or not. The twenty-five dollars is payable in advance."

The blind man opened his shirt, unbuckled his belt.

"What is this?" Bertha asked. "A strip tease?"

"A money belt," he explained.

Bertha watched him while he pushed a thumb and finger down into the well-filled pockets of a bulging money belt. He brought out a thick package of folded bills, took one from the outside, and handed it to Bertha. "Just give me the change," he said. "Never mind the receipt."

It was a one-hundred-dollar bill.

"Have you," Bertha asked, "got anything smaller?"

The blind man answered her with a single monosyllable. "No."

Bertha Cool opened her purse, took out a key, unlocked a drawer in her desk, pulled out a steel cashbox, slipped a key from a cord around her neck, opened the cashbox, and took out seven ten-dollar bills and a five.

"How and where do you want your reports?" she asked.

"I want them made orally," he said, "since I can't read. Just stop by the bank building and report progress. Lean over and speak in a low voice. Be careful no one's listening. You can pretend you're looking at a necktie."

"Okay," Bertha said.

The blind man got up, picked up his cane, and, with the tip, explored his way to the door. Abruptly he stopped, turned, and said, "I've partially retired. If the weather isn't nice, I won't be working."

Chapter Two

BERTHA COOL glared down at Elsie Brand, taking her indignation out on the stenographer.

"Can you beat that?" she demanded. "The guy pulls open his shirt, unbuttons his pants, and has a money belt wrapped around him that looks like a spare tire. He opens one of the pockets, pulls out a bunch of bills, and peels off one. It's a century. I ask him has he got anything smaller, and he says no."

Elsie Brand seemed to see nothing peculiar about that.

"A guy," Bertha Cool said, "who sits down on the sidewalk, doesn't have to pay any rent, has no taxes, no employees, and doesn't have to make out a lot of social security reports. He has a money belt strapped around him that has a fortune in it. *I* have to change that hundred, and it takes damn near every cent in my cashbox. And then," and Bertha Cool's voice rose to a high pitch of emotion, "and then, mind you, he turns around at the door and says that he won't be working unless the weather is good. *I've* never been able to stay in bed on those cold, rainy mornings—or when there's a damp, slimy fog. *I* get out and slosh my way up to the office, splashing around through puddles, getting my ankles soaking wet, and—"

"Yes," Elsie Brand said, "I do the same thing. Only I have to get here an hour earlier than you do, Mrs. Cool, and if *I* had to change a hundred-dollar bill, I'd—"

"All right, all right," Bertha Cool interrupted quickly, sensing that the conversation had turned on dangerous ground, and that Elsie Brand might be going to mention quite casually the high wages that were being paid government stenographers. "Never mind that end of it. Skip it. I just stopped by to tell you that I'm going to be out for a while. I'm going to find a girl who was hurt in an automobile accident."

7

"Going to handle it yourself?" Elsie Brand asked.

Bertha Cool all but snorted. "Why should I pay an operative," she asked, "to go out on a simple little thing like that? The girl was hurt when an automobile ran into her at the corner, last Friday night at a quarter to six. The man who ran into her took her to a hospital. All I've got to do is to drift down to the traffic department, get a report on the accident, take a streetcar out to the hospital, ask the girl how she's feeling, and then report to this blind man."

"And why does *he* want the information?" Elsie asked.

"Yes," Bertha Cool said sarcastically, "why does he? He just wants to know where the little dear is, so he can send her flowers, because she brought sweetness and light into his life. He liked to hear her feet tripping along the sidewalk, and he misses her now she's gone, so he pays me twenty-five bucks to find the little darling. Phooey!"

"You don't believe it?" Elsie Brand asked.

"No," Bertha said shortly. "I don't believe it. *I'm* not the type. *You* might believe that it's all being done for sweet charity. Bertha Cool doesn't believe fairy stories. Bertha Cool believes twenty-five bucks. She's going to earn it in just about an hour and a half. So if anyone comes in and wants anything, find out what it is and make an appointment for right after lunch—if it looks as though there's any money in it. If it's someone soliciting contributions for anything—and I don't give a damn what it is—I'm out of town."

Bertha strode across the office, slamming the door viciously behind her, noting with satisfaction that the keyboard of Elsie Brand's typewriter exploded into noise almost before the door was closed.

At the traffic department, however, Bertha got her first jolt. There was no report whatever of an accident at that street intersection on the date and hour named.

"That's a hell of a note," Bertha complained to the man in charge of the records. "Here a man smacks into a girl, and you don't know a thing about it."

"Many times motorists fail to make reports," the officer

explained patiently. "*We* can't make 'em. The law requires they must do so. Whenever there's an officer within a reasonable distance, he notes the license number, and we check to see that the report is made out and filed by the motorist."

"And you mean to say that at an intersection like this, there wasn't a traffic officer within earshot?"

"At that intersection," the man explained, "the traffic officer goes off duty at five-forty, and walks two blocks over to the main boulevard to help handle traffic there. We're shorthanded, and we have to do the best we can."

"You listen to me," Bertha Cool demanded. "I'm a taxpayer. I'm entitled to this information. I want it."

"We'd like very much to help you get it."

"Well, how *am* I going to find out about it?"

"You might call the hospitals and ask them if a patient was received for an examination some time between six and seven o'clock last Friday night. I take it you can describe the patient?"

"Generally."

"You don't know her name?"

"No."

The traffic officer shook his head. "Well, you might try it."

Bertha tried it, sweating in the confines of a telephone booth, reluctantly dropping coins into a pay telephone. After having expended thirty-five cents, her patience was worn thin. She had explained and re-explained, only to be told, "Just a moment," and be connected with some other department to whom she had to explain all over again.

At the end of her list she was out thirty-five cents and had no information, which hardly improved her irascible disposition.

Chapter Three

TRAFFIC RUMBLED past the busy intersection at the corner. Pedestrians returning from lunch streamed across the street in intermittent rivulets of moving humanity. The bells on the automatic block signals clanged with monotonous regularity at fixed intervals. Occasional streetcars grinding past to the accompaniment of clanging gongs added to the noise of automobile traffic, the clashing of gears, the sound of engines as they were intermittently speeded up or braked to a stop.

The day was warm and sunny, and the smell of exhaust gases clung to the concrete canyon of the street in a sticky vapor.

Kosling sat in a little patch of shade in front of the bank building, his legs doubled under him, his stock of neckties displayed in a tray suspended by a strap from his shoulders. Over on the left on a smaller tray were the lead pencils. At occasional intervals a coin jangled into the tin cup. Less frequently someone stopped to look at the assortment of ties.

Kosling knew his merchandise by a sense of touch and a keen memory for its position on the tray. "Now this tie is very nice for a young man, madam," he would proclaim, touching a vivid bit of red silk, splashed with white and crossed with black stripes. "Over here is something very nice in a deep blue, and here's a checkered effect which would make a splendid gift. Here's something that goes very nicely with a sport outfit, and—"

He broke off as his ears heard the pound of Bertha Cool's determined feet on the sidewalk.

"Yes, ma'am, I think you'll be satisfied with that one. Yes, ma'am, fifty cents is all. Just drop it in the cup, please. Thank you."

Because the man couldn't see, he didn't look up as Bertha bent over the tray. "Well?" he asked.

Bertha bent down. "No progress," she said, "as yet."

The blind man sat patiently waiting for more, saying nothing.

Bertha hesitated a moment before deciding on an explanation. "I've checked the traffic records and called the hospitals. There hasn't been a thing. I've got to have more information to go on."

10

Kosling answered in the quiet, flat monotone of one who has nothing to gain by impressing his personality upon his listeners. "I'd done all that before I came to you."

"You had!" Bertha exclaimed. "Why in hell didn't you say so?"

"You didn't think I'd pay twenty-five dollars just to get someone to run an errand, did you?"

"You didn't tell me you'd done that," Bertha exclaimed indignantly.

"You didn't tell me that you intended to do the stuff anybody could do. I thought I was hiring a detective."

Bertha straightened, went pounding away, her face flushed eyes glittering, feet swollen in her shoes from contact with the hot sidewalk.

Elsie Brand looked up as Bertha came in. "Any luck?"

Bertha shook her head and marched on into the inner office where she banged the door shut and sat down to think things over.

Her cogitations resulted in an advertisement to be placed in the personal columns of the daily papers.

Persons who saw accident at corner of Crestlake and Broadway last Friday at about quarter to six please communicate with B. Cool, Drexel Building. No annoyance, no trouble, no subpoena. Simply want to get information. Reward of $5.00 paid for license number of automobile which struck young woman.

Bertha settled back in the swivel chair, looked the copy over, consulted the classified rates, and started crossing words out with her pencil.

As finally completed, the ad read:

Witnesses accident Crestlake Broadway Friday communicate B. Cool, Drexel Building. $3.00 reward license number.

Bertha studied that ad for a moment, then, with her pencil, crossed out the word *three-dollar* and wrote *two-dollar* in its place.

"Two dollars is quite enough," she said to herself. "And besides, no one would have remembered the license number unless he'd written it down; and if he wrote it down, he is the kind who would like to be a witness. Two dollars is quite enough for him."

Chapter Four

It was Wednesday afternoon when Elsie Brand opened the door of Bertha Cool's private office. "A gentleman outside won't give his name."

"What's he want?"

"Says you put an ad in the paper."

"About what?"

"Automobile accident."

"So what?" Bertha Cool asked.

"He wants to collect two dollars."

Bertha Cool's eyes glittered. "Show him in."

The man whom Elsie Brand escorted into Bertha Cool's private office seemed to be trying to get through life by expending the least possible effort. He had a semi-pretzel posture as though neck, shoulders, hips, and legs all seemed afraid they would support more than their fair share of the weight, and even the cigarette which he held in his mouth drooped nonchalantly, bobbing up and down when he talked.

"Hello," he said. "This the place that wanted information about the automobile accident?"

Bertha Cool beamed at him. "That's right," she said. "Won't you sit down? Have that chair—no, not that one, it's not so comfortable. Take this one over by the window. That's it; it's cooler there. What's your name?"

The man grinned at her.

He was somewhere in the middle thirties, around five foot-nine, slightly underweight; he had an indolent motion, a sallow complexion, and eyes that were bright with impudence. "Don't think for a minute," he said, "that anybody's going to slap a subpoena on me and say, 'Now you're a witness, and what are you going to do about it?' There's a lot of talk that has to take place before that happens."

"What kind of talk?" Bertha asked, carefully fitting a cigarette into her long, carved ivory holder.

"The kind of talk that starts in with a discussion of what's in it for me," the man said.

Bertha smiled affably. "Well, now, perhaps I can fix things so there'll be a good deal in it for you—*if* you saw what I am hoping you saw."

"Make no mistake, sister. I saw it all. You know how it is; some people don't want to be witnesses, and you can't blame them. Somebody slaps them with a subpoena. They go up to court five times, and learn that the lawyers have continued the case. The sixth time there's another trial going on, and they wait two days before their case comes up. Then a lot of lawyers throw questions at 'em and make monkeys of 'em. When the case is finished, the lawyer sticks his mitt out and tells 'em he's much obliged, and coughs up a check for ten or fifteen bucks witness fees. The guy's testimony gave him the break that resulted in a verdict of fifteen grand, but the lawyer soaks the client fifty per cent of it. It's the witness that's the sucker. *My* mother didn't have any foolish children."

"I can see she didn't," Bertha beamed at him. "You're just exactly the type of man I like to deal with."

"That's swell. Go ahead and deal."

Bertha said, "I'm particularly interested in finding out something about the identity of—"

"Wait a minute," the man interrupted. "Don't begin in the middle. Let's go back to the beginning."

"But I *am* beginning at the beginning."

"Oh, no, you're not. Take it easy now, sister. The first thing that little Willie wants to know is what's in it for him."

"I'm trying to explain it to little Willie," Bertha said, and smiled coyly.

"Then get your checkbook open, and we'll have the proper background."

Bertha said. "Perhaps you didn't read the ad right."

"Perhaps *you* didn't write it right."

13

Bertha said, with a burst of sudden inspiration, "Look here, I'm not representing either of the parties to the accident."

Her visitor seemed crestfallen. "You're not?"

"No."

"Then what's your angle?"

"I just want to find out where the girl is who was hurt."

He grinned at her, and his grin was a leer filled with cynical understanding.

"Oh, no," Bertha said, "it isn't like that. I don't care anything at all about what happens after I find her. I'm not going to steer her to any lawyer. I don't care whether she sues him for damages or whether she doesn't, whether she recovers or whether she doesn't. I just want to know where I can find her."

"Why?"

"On another matter," Bertha said.

"Oh, yeah?"

"That's the truth."

"Then I guess you're not the party I want to talk with."

"Have you," Bertha said, "got the license number of the car that hit her?"

"I told you I had everything. Listen, lady, when a piece of luck drops into my lap, I'm all ready with the little old pencil and the notebook. See? I've got it all down; how it happened, the license number of the automobile—the whole works." He pulled a notebook from his pocket, opened it, and showed Bertha a page scribbled with notes. "This ain't the first accident I've seen." he said, and then added ruefully. *"I'll* say it ain't! The first accident I stuck my neck out and told what happened. The insurance company paid the lawyer ten grand. I didn't go to court. The lawyer thanked me, shook hands with me, told me I was a fine citizen. Get it? *I* was a fine citizen. The lawyer got the ten grand. He split with the client. I got a handshake. Well, handshakes don't mean that much to me. After that I got wise. I carry my little notebook, and I don't testify to anything until after we've had a little get-together talk. But don't worry about my not having the information. Whenever I see anything, I have all the dope on it. That little note-book comes in handy. Get me?"

"I get you," Bertha said, "but you're at the wrong place. You're talking to the wrong person."

"How come?"

Bertha said, "A man wants me to locate this woman. He doesn't even know her name. He was becoming at-tached to her, and then she was smashed out of his life."

The man took the cigarette from his mouth, flicked the ashes off onto Bertha Cool's carpet, threw back his head, and laughed.

A slow flush of indignation began to color Bertha's beefy neck. "I'm glad you think it's funny," she snapped.

"Funny? It's a scream! Boy, oh boy! Ha, ha, ha! He just wants to send the little lady a valentine, and doesn't know where to send it. 'Have you got the license number of the car that hit her?' "

"Don't you see?" Bertha asked. "The man who struck her was going to take her to a hospital. My client wants to know what hospital she went to."

The man in the big, comfortable, overstuffed chair by the window where it was cool writhed with laughter. He doubled up, slapped his leg, became red in the face. "Ha, ha, ha! Lady, you slay me! You're a card. I mean you really *are* a card!"

He took a handkerchief from his pocket, wiped his per-spiring forehead and his eyes. "Boy, oh, boy, that's spreading it on. What I mean, it's spreading it on with a trowel. Tell me, lady, do you find many of them that fall for that sort of stuff? I'm just interested, because when people get *that* easy, there's always a chance for someone to make a little something out of it."

Bertha pushed back her chair. "All right," she said angrily. "Now listen to me, you little smart pip-squeak. You're brainy, aren't you? You're mamma's smart little boy. You were the bright one of the family. You're the

15

clever guy. All the rest of them are suckers. What's it got you? Look at you. With a twenty-five-dollar ready-made suit, a dollar necktie, a shirt that's got holes in it where the edges of the collar rub against it, a pair of shoes that are run-down at the heels. Smart, eh? Wise guy! You're half smart, just smart enough to stand in your own light and kick because there's always a shadow tailing you. All right, Mr. Smartypants, now let *me* tell *you* something."

Bertha was on her feet now, leaning across the desk.

"Since you're so damn smart, my client is a blind man, a blind beggar who sits down on the corner and sells pencils and neckties. He's got to the age where he's sentimental, and this little wren stopped and passed the time of day with him, gave him a pat on the back and cheered him up. He's worried about her because she didn't come to work Monday, and she didn't come to work Tuesday. He asked me to try and locate her for him; and because he's just a sweet old codger, Bertha falls for his song and takes on the job at about the quarter the price I'd charge a regular client.

"I was going to try and give you a break. If you'd given me the information I wanted, I was going to steer things around so that if a lawyer picked it up, you could cash in. Now, you're so damned smart, you just go ahead and find your own lawyer."

The man in the chair had ceased laughing. He wasn't even smiling. He looked at Bertha Cool with a puzzled, half-dazed expression in which there was some anger, some surprise.

"Go on," Bertha said. "Get the hell out of here, before I throw you out."

She started marching around the desk.

"Now, wait a minute, lady. I—"

"Out!" Bertha shouted.

The man jumped up out of the chair as though he had been sitting on a cushion of pins. "Now, wait a minute, lady. Maybe you and me can really do business."

"Not by a damn sight," Bertha said. "I'm not going to soil my hands playing around with a cheap, two-bit, penny-ante, race-track tout. You're so damned smart, go find yourself the lawyer that *wants* your information."

"Well, perhaps—"

Bertha Cool came down on him like an avalanche. Her capable right hand caught a handful of slack cloth in the back of his coat, twisted it into a knot. Her arm shot out straight, and her sturdy legs started marching.

Elsie Brand looked up in surprise as they tore through the outer office.

The outer door slammed with a concussion that jarred the frosted glass. Bertha Cool glared at the door for a second or two, then turned to Elsie Brand's desk. "All right, Elsie, after him. We'll teach the chiseler!"

"I don't get you," Elsie said.

Bertha grabbed the back of the stenographic chair, sent it spinning and skidding halfway across the floor before Elsie Brand could get up.

"Follow him! Find out who he is and where he goes. If he has a car, get the license number. On your way! Hurry!"

Elsie Brand started for the door.

"Wait until he gets in the elevator," Bertha cautioned. "Don't ride down in the same elevator with him. Pick him up on the street."

Elsie Brand hurried through the door.

Bertha Cool pushed the typewriter chair back in front of Elsie's stenographic desk, marched back into her own office, picked up the half-burned cigarette in the holder, fitted it to her lips, and dropped into the big swivel chair.

She was puffing slightly from her exertion.

"That little bastard," she muttered to herself. "Joining the Navy! God, how I miss him! *He'd* have handled that without any fuss."

Chapter Five

ELSIE BRAND was back within thirty minutes. "Get him?" Bertha Cool asked.

Elsie Brand shook her head. A frown of annoyance crossed Bertha Cool's forehead. "Why not?"

"Because," Elsie Brand said, "I'm not Donald Lam. I'm not a detective; I'm a stenographer. What's more, I think he was wise to me all the way."

"What did he do?"

"Walked down to the corner, stopped in front of the blind man who's our client, and dropped silver dollars into the cup—five of them."

"Bowed his head every time a dollar hit the tin cup, and said, 'Thank you, brother.' He said it five times, very seriously and with considerable dignity."

"And then?" Bertha asked.

"Then he crossed the street, started walking very fast. I stretched my legs, trying to keep up with him. He kept going until he caught a signal just as it was changing. Then he scooted across the street. I tried to follow him. The cop pushed me back, gave me a bawling out. A streetcar came along, and my man was gone."

Bertha Cool said, "You should have gone after the streetcar and—"

"Wait a minute," Elsie Brand interrupted. "A taxicab was standing halfway down the block. I made frantic signals, and the driver came up. I climbed aboard and had the cab driver pass the streetcar three times. Every time we went past, I studied the passengers. I couldn't see our man on the streetcar, so then I had the cab driver take me ahead of the streetcar for two blocks and stop. I paid him off and caught the streetcar as it came along. Our man wasn't aboard."

Bertha said, with deep feeling, "Fry me for an oyster."

Chapter Six

IT WAS exactly nine minutes before five o'clock when Elsie Brand opened the door of Bertha Cool's private office. She was quite evidently trying to keep excitement from her demeanor until after the door had been closed behind her. Then she said breathlessly, "He's back."

"Who's back?"

"That witness who saw the accident."

Bertha Cool gave that thoughtful consideration for several seconds before she said, "He wants to give in. He's a dirty, damn blackmailer. I shouldn't even give him the satisfaction of seeing him."

Elsie Brand waited, saying nothing.

"All right," Bertha said, "send him in."

The man was smiling and affable as he entered the office. "Rather crude," he said, "that shadowing job you tried on me. No hard feelings, eh, Mrs. Cool?"

Bertha didn't say anything.

"I've been thinking things over," the man went on. "Perhaps you *were* telling the truth. I'm going to make you a deal. The girl doesn't know who hit her. I guess I'm about the only one who does. Now, that information isn't doing *me* any good locked up in my notebook so I'm going to give you the girl's name and address. It won't cost you a cent. Go see her. Talk with her. She's got a swell cause of action. Twenty-five per cent is what I want."

"Twenty-five per cent of what?" Bertha asked.

"Of what she gets from the man who was driving the car. He's probably insured. There'll be a settlement."

"I don't have anything to do with that," Bertha said. "I told you that before."

"I know. You *told* me that. No argument about that. Forewarned is forearmed. But *I'm* telling *you* that if she wants to find out who hit her, it's going to cost her a fat slice of her settlement. I'll have a lawyer draw up an agreement all shipshape. Is it a deal?"

Bertha Cool clamped her lips together, shook her head with dogged obstinacy.

Her visitor laughed. "Don't kid me. Of course, it's a deal. You may not be interested in the lawsuit *now*, but you will be after you think it over. Well, you can always get me by putting an ad in the personal column."

"What's your name?"

"Opportunity—Mr. John Q. Opportunity."

Bertha Cool said, "I tell you—"

"Yes, yes, I know," he interrupted smoothly. "The girl you want is Josephine Dell. She lives in the Bluebonnet Apartments on South Figueroa Street. She didn't go to a hospital at all."

"Why not?" Bertha asked. "The man was going to take her to a hospital."

"That's right," her visitor said. "He was going to. He wanted to see that she was examined by a doctor so that he'd know she wasn't hurt, but for some reason she didn't. The accident was Friday night. Saturday morning she woke up feeling stiff and sore. She telephoned the place where she worked and was told to stay home that day. Sunday she stayed in bed. She could get a few hundred for a settlement—but she doesn't know who hit her."

The man got up, lighted a cigarette, took a deep drag. His droop-lidded eyes regarded Bertha Cool speculatively. "Now," he said, "you see where I come in."

Bertha Cool glanced toward the door, started to say something, then checked herself.

Her visitor smiled. "Going to make the old crack about where I go out, I suppose, and caught yourself in time. After all, Mrs. Cool, you can't very well get along without me. Well, I'll be rambling along. No charge for that information. It's what you might call a free sample of my wares. When you want to get the information that will make real money, let me know. Good afternoon." He sauntered on out of the office.

Bertha was ready for the street within ten seconds of the time the door had closed on her departing visitor.

Elsie Brand was closing up her typewriter desk as Bertha Cool came out of the other office. She glanced at her employer curiously, seemed on the point of asking whether Bertha had acquired the desired information, then apparently changed her mind. Bertha Cool volunteered no information.

The Bluebonnet Apartments was a typical Southern California apartment building containing, for the most part, single apartments renting from twenty-seven-fifty to forty dollars a month. The sides were covered with brick. The front had a white stucco finish with little ornamental roofs projecting a few feet over doorways and windows. These roofs were covered with conventional red tile. The building was fifty feet wide and three stories in height. There was no lobby, and a list of names and buttons on the outside of the front door flanked the mailboxes.

Bertha Cool ran her eye down the list of names, catching that of Josephine Dell about midway in the column. Bertha's competent, pudgy forefinger speared the button. She picked the earpiece from the hook, listened.

A young woman's voice said, "Who is it, please?"

"A woman who wants to see you about your accident."

The voice said, "All right," and a few seconds later, the electric release on the door catch buzzed a signal for Bertha to enter.

It was a walk-up, and Bertha climbed the stairs with the slow deliberation of one who is determined to conserve wind and energy, leaning slightly forward as she negotiated the steps, getting her legs upward, giving to her climb a peculiar jerky motion. She arrived at the apartment, however, without being out of breath, and her knuckles pounded authoritatively on the door.

The young woman who opened the door was about twenty-five. She had red hair, an upturned nose, laughing eyes and a mouth which seemed naturally inclined toward smiles.

"Hello."

"Hello." Bertha said. "You're Josephine Dell?"

"Yes."

"May I come in?"

"Come right ahead."

Josephine Dell was dressed in a lounging robe, pajamas, and slippers. The interior of the modest apartment indicated she had been confined to her room for some time. There was a litter of newspapers and magazines. The ash tray was well filled, and there was an odor of stale cigarette smoke clinging to the apartment.

"Sit down," the young woman said. "Tomorrow I get my release."

"You've been laid up?" Bertha asked.

"Under observation," Josephine Dell said, and laughed. "Misfortunes never come singly."

Bertha Cool adjusted herself comfortably in the chair. "There's been something else besides your automobile accident?" she asked.

"Of course. Didn't you know?"

"No."

"I'm out of a job."

"You mean you were discharged because you couldn't get to work?"

"Good heavens, no! It was when Mr. Milbers passed away that my troubles started. I presumed you knew about that. But suppose you tell me who *you* are and what you want before we start talking."

Bertha said, "I'm not from any insurance company. I can't offer you a cent."

Josephine Dell's face showed disappointment. "I was hoping that you represented some insurance company."

"I thought perhaps you were."

"You see, when the man hit me, I didn't think I was hurt at all. It gave me a pretty good shaking-up, of course, but, good heavens, I was always trained to take things in my stride; and just as soon as I could catch my breath, I kept saying to myself, 'Now, don't be a crybaby. After all, there are no bones broken. You just got knocked over.' "

Bertha nodded sympathetically.

"And this young man was *so* nice. He was out of his automobile in a flash. He had his arm around me and was putting me into the car almost before I knew it. He kept insisting that I must go to a hospital at least for a checkup. I laughed at the idea, and then it occurred to me perhaps he was doing it for his own protection, so I told him all right, I'd go. Well, after we got started, we began to chat, and I think I convinced him that I wasn't hurt at all, and there wasn't going to be any claim for

22

damages. I told him I wasn't going to even claim a dime. So he consented to take me home."

Bertha's nod was the sympathetic gesture which keeps confidences pouring out.

"Then after I thought I was all right, I began to develop peculiar symptoms. I called a doctor and found out it's not at all unusual in cases of a concussion for a person apparently to be all right for a day or so, and then have very serious symptoms develop. The doctor seems to think I'm lucky to be here at all."

Again Bertha nodded.

"And," Josephine Dell went on, with a little laugh, "I didn't even take the man's license number. I didn't get his name and haven't the faintest idea of who he is. Not that I want to stick him, but if he's insured, I certainly could use a few dollars right now."

"Yes," Bertha said, "I can appreciate that. Well, if you want to find out who he is, there's a possibility that—"

"Yes?" Josephine Dell asked as Bertha caught herself.

"Nothing," Bertha said.

"Suppose you tell me just what is *your* connection with the case?"

Bertha Cool handed her a card. "I'm the head of a detective agency," she said.

"A detective!" Josephine Dell exclaimed in surprise.

"Yes."

Josephine Dell laughed. "I always thought detectives were sinister people. You seem very human."

"I am."

"Why on earth are *you* interested in *me?*"

"Because someone hired me to find you."

"Who?"

Bertha smiled and said, "You'd never guess, not in a hundred years. This is a man who is interested in you. He knew that you were hurt and wanted to find out how you were getting along."

"But why on earth didn't he ring up—"

"He didn't know where to reach you."

"You mean he didn't know where I was working?"

"That's right."

"Who is it?"

"An older man," Bertha said. "A man who seems to—"

"Oh, I'll bet it was the blind man!"

Bertha seemed somewhat chagrined that Josephine Dell had guessed the identity of her client so easily. "How did you know?"

"I didn't, except that you seemed so confident I'd never think who it was that I realized it must be someone rather unusual. You know, I think a lot of him. I was thinking about him only today, wondering how I could let him know that I was getting along all right." She laughed and went on. "You just can't write a letter addressed to the blind man who sells neckties in front of a bank building, can you?"

"Hardly," Bertha said.

"Will you tell him how very, very much I appreciate his interest?"

Bertha nodded.

"Tell him that it means a lot to me. I'll probably see him myself tomorrow morning or the day after if there aren't any further complications. I think he's a *dear*."

"He seems very fond of you," Bertha said. "Rather an unusual type—very observant."

"Well, you tell him for me that I'm all right, and that I sent my love. Will you do that?"

"I certainly will."

Bertha rose from her chair, then hesitated for a moment. "I *might* be able to do something about—well, about compensation for you, but I'd have to spend some money finding out who ran into you. I wouldn't want to do it unless you felt there was no other way."

"You mean *you* could find out who ran into me?"

"I think I might. It would cost some money."

"How much?"

"I don't know. Probably a percentage of what you'd get. I'd say offhand it would cost half of what you'd get. I wouldn't want you to do it if there were any other way."

24

"And you could handle the whole thing for me?"

"If there was a settlement, yes. If it went to court, that, of course, would be different."

"Oh, I know it won't go to court. This young man was *so* nice and *so* considerate. I feel confident that he's insured, and if he had any idea I was laid up—but then, it isn't anything serious. I've only lost three or four days from work, and my job was finished anyway."

"You were working for a man who died?"

"Yes. Harlow Milbers."

"Your office must have been close to the place where the blind man hangs out."

"About two blocks from the bank—in that goofy old-time studio building around the corner. Mr. Milbers had a little studio up there."

"What did he do?"

"Research work in connection with a private hobby of his. He had a theory that all military campaigns follow certain lines, that defense is of no value against aggression until aggression has expended itself past a certain point, that no country can ever achieve anything permanent through aggression because once you start aggression, there's no place to stop. No matter how much force you have or how much initial impetus, you eventually arrive at a point where you're vulnerable. The more powerful you are at the start, the farther your conquests take you, and the more extended your fronts are—but then you're not interested in all that."

"It's an interesting theory," Bertha said.

"He was going to write a book on it, and he dictated a lot of notes to me. It was a nice job."

Bertha said, "Well, if you decide you want to do something about that automobile accident, let me know. I presume you can get five hundred or a thousand. There's nerve shock, you know, and—"

"Oh, I wouldn't want a thing for the nerve shock, just for the loss of time and my doctor's bills."

"Well, of course," Bertha explained, "when you start collecting from an insurance company, there are certain expenses involved, and people usually try to get all they can, so that enough will be left after they pay expenses. But think it over, dearie. You have my card, and you can always get in touch with me."

"You're very kind, Mrs. Cool. Saturday and Sunday didn't count, so I've only lost three days, so far. I get thirty a week, so the three days would amount to eighteen dollars, and the doctor charged seven. I'd want to collect twenty-five dollars from the insurance company."

Bertha paused, her hand on the knob of the door. She said, "Don't be a dope—" when knuckles sounded on the outside, a somewhat timid, venturesome knock.

Josephine Dell said, "Open it please."

Bertha Cool opened the door.

A mild-mannered, little man of fifty-seven or -eight, with a sandy mustache, slightly stooped shoulders, and blue eyes smiled at her. "You're Miss Dell, aren't you? I'm Christopher Milbers. I got through the outer door because I rang the wrong apartment. I'm sorry. I should have gone back out after I realized my mistake. I wanted to talk with you about my cousin. It was so sudden—"

"Not me," Bertha said, standing to one side so that the man could see past her into the room. "*This* is Miss Dell. I was just calling on her."

"Oh," the man said apologetically.

"Come on in," Josephine Dell called. "I won't get up if you don't mind, Mr. Milbers. I've been in an automobile accident. Nothing serious, but the doctor told me not to get up and down any more than necessary. I really feel that I know you. I've written quite a few letters to you at your cousin's dictation."

Milbers entered the room, beamed at Josephine Dell, and said solicitously, "You've been in an accident?"

She gave him her hand. "Just a minor accident. Do sit down."

Bertha said, "Well, I'll be going," and started across the threshold.

"Just a moment, Mrs. Cool," Josephine Dell said. "I think I'd like to talk with you some more about getting a settlement. Could you wait just a few moments?"

Bertha said, "I've really told you all I have to say. Only don't be silly about the damages. If you want to go ahead with a really worth-while claim, get in touch with me. My telephone number's on my card."

"All right. Thank you, I will."

Chapter Seven

SITTING IN the early-morning sunlight, his back against the granite blocks of the bank building, the blind man seemed even more frail than he had when Bertha Cool had seen him on the occasion of her previous report.

Bertha Cool tried to fool him as she approached by changing the tempo of her steps.

He said, without looking up, "Hello, Mrs. Cool."

She laughed. "Thought I might fool you by changing my steps."

"You can't change the distinguishing features," he said. "I knew you were walking differently, but I knew who it was. Have you found out anything?"

"Yes, I've located her."

"Tell me, is she all right?"

"Yes."

"You're certain? She wasn't badly hurt?"

"No, she's all right now."

"You have the address?"

"The Bluebonnet Apartments on Figueroa. She was working for a man who died."

"Who was he?"

"A man named Milbers. He was a writer. Had some theory on history he was trying to incorporate into a book when he died."

"The office was near here?" the blind man asked.

"Yes. Around the corner of the next block in the old loft building."

"I remember the place—I mean what it looks like. It was there before I went blind."

There was silence for a moment. Kosling seemed to be

searching his memory as though trying to dig up some half-forgotten fact. Abruptly, he said, "I'll bet I know who he was."

"Who?"

"Her boss. He must have been the old man with the cane who walked with that peculiar dragging shuffle of the right foot. I've often wondered about him. It's been about a week since I last heard him going past. A man who kept very much to himself. Been going past here for over a year now, but he's never spoken to me, never dropped anything in the cup. Yes, that must have been Milbers. You say he's dead?"

"Yes."

"How did he die?"

"I don't know. The girl told me he died. I gathered it was rather sudden."

The blind man nodded his head. "He wasn't in good health. That dragging of the right foot kept getting worse, particularly the last month or six weeks. You told her how you happened to be looking for her?"

"Yes," Bertha said. "You didn't tell me not to, and I thought it was all right. She kept thinking I was representing the insurance company and was going to offer to make a settlement for the automobile accident, so I told her about how I happened to be employed. It was all right, wasn't it?"

"It was all right. How do we stand on money?"

"All square," Bertha said. "You've given me twenty-five bucks, and that's the amount of my bill. Twenty-five dollars. I didn't have any expenses."

"All right, thank you. Now that you've got to know me, I hope you'll stop and pass the time of day with me when you're coming by. I miss your partner very much. You haven't heard anything from him, have you?"

"No."

"I'd appreciate it very much if you'd let me know when you do."

"All right, I will. Well, good luck."

Bertha moved on down the street to the entrance of

her office building, went up in the elevator, and heard Elsie Brand clacking away on the typewriter. She opened the door of the entrance office, said, "Hello, Elsie. I just—" and stopped in the middle of the sentence.

The tall man with the droopy eyes and the pendulant cigarette was sitting slouched in an easy chair, his ankles crossed in front of him, his hands thrust down into his trousers pockets. He looked up with impudent appraisal at Bertha Cool and said, "How did you come out?"

"What do you mean?"

"You know what I mean. Did you get the job of shaking down the insurance company?"

Bertha said, "That wasn't what I went for."

"I know, I know. How about it? Do we make a deal or not?"

Bertha said, "I tell you I hardly mentioned it."

"I understand. Twenty-five per cent. Is it a deal?"

Bertha said irritably, "You don't listen when I tell you in English. I guess I'll have to learn Chinese, and see if you understand that any better."

"It'd be the same in any language," he told her.

Bertha said, "I'll take a gamble with you. I'll pay you twenty-five dollars cash money for the information."

He laughed at her.

"Well, that's all there is to it," Bertha said. "I'd be paying that out of my own pocket, because she hasn't hired me to do anything with the insurance company. Anyway, she wouldn't want to stick 'em on a settlement, just her doctor's bill and compensation for the time she's lost. She figures the total at twenty-five dollars."

"That's what *she* wants?"

"That's right."

"You'd educate her, of course."

Bertha said, "I probably won't have anything to do with it."

"Maybe the insurance company would like to buy my notebook."

"Perhaps it would. Why don't you try it?"

"I may at that."

"You probably have."

"No, I'm strictly on the up-and-up. I wouldn't alter my testimony for anyone. That's why I didn't go to this girl direct and get a cut from her. Some lawyer would smoke out what I'd done and raise the devil with me. But some private, confidential arrangement with *you* would be different. Then when some mouthpiece asks me if the plaintiff has offered to pay me anything, I'd just look wise and say, 'The usual witness fees is all.' "

Bertha laughed cynically. "Twenty-five dollars," she announced, "is the limit of what she'll ask at present, and that's my limit to you. I'll take that much of a gamble."

"Twenty-five per cent," he insisted.

"I tell you there isn't anything to get a cut from—not as yet."

"All right, perhaps things will look up later."

"Look here," Bertha asked. "where can I get in touch with you?"

He said, grinning, "You can't," and sauntered out of the office.

Bertha glowered at the door as it closed behind him. "Damn him," she said. "I'd like to slap him right across the mouth."

"Why don't you?" Elsie Brand asked curiously.

"I've probably got to play ball with him," Bertha said.

"You mean, accept his proposition?"

"Eventually—if I can't get a better one."

"Why?" Elsie Brand asked curiously. "Why do you get mixed up with people of that stripe, particularly when you don't like them?"

"Because there's money in it," Bertha said, and strode across the office to closet herself with the morning newspaper in her private office.

She was halfway through the sporting sheet when the telephone buzzed on her desk. Bertha picked up the receiver, and Elsie Brand said, "Have you time to give a few minutes to a Christopher Milbers? He says that he's met you."

"Milbers—Milbers?" Bertha repeated the name a couple of times, then said suddenly, "Oh, yes, I place him now. What does *he* want?"

"He didn't say."

"Tell him to come in."

Christopher Milbers seemed even more self-effacing in Bertha Cool's office than he had in Josephine Dell's apartment. "I hope I'm not disturbing you," he said apologetically.

"What is it you wanted?" Bertha asked.

"Miss Dell told me that you were a detective. I was astounded."

"We make confidential investigations," Bertha said.

"A detective sounds so much more romantic than an investigator—don't you think so?"

Bertha fixed him with a cold eye. "There isn't any romance in this business. It's a job, and I have an overhead just like any business. What do *you* want?"

Milbers said, "I'd like to employ you. I don't know what your rates are."

"It depends on the nature of the job and the amount of money involved." Her eyes were showing keen interest now.

"You wouldn't mind," Milbers asked, "if I take the time to tell you the story from the beginning?"

"Go ahead."

"Well, my cousin Harlow was rather eccentric."

"I gathered as much."

"He was very much of an individual. He wanted to live his own life in his own way. He didn't want to be dictated to or dominated. His attitude toward his relatives was always rather—shall we say colored—by that attitude."

Christopher Milbers raised his hands, opened the fingers far apart, and placed the tips together, pointed upward toward his chin. He looked at Bertha Cool over the upturned finger tips as though pathetically anxious to make certain she got exactly the point he was trying to make.

31

"Married?" Bertha Cool asked.

"His wife died ten years ago."

"No children?"

"No."

"You're the only relative?"

"Yes."

"How about the funeral? Who had charge of that?"

"The funeral is tomorrow. I'm having it here. I didn't get the telegram announcing his death until Monday night. I was out of town, and there was some delay in getting the telegram to me. I trust you appreciate the delicacy of the decision that was then thrust upon me— as to the funeral?"

Bertha said, "I don't know a damn thing about funerals. What do you want to see me about?"

"Yes, yes, I'm coming to that. I've told you that my cousin was eccentric."

"Yes."

"Among other things, he had no confidence whatever in the economic security of established business."

A spasm of expression crossed Bertha Cool's face. "Hell!" she said. "That isn't eccentricity. That's sense."

Christopher Milbers pressed his hands together until the fingers arched backward at the knuckles. "Eccentricity or sense, whatever you wish to call it, Mrs. Cool, my cousin always kept a large sum of currency in his possession –in a billfold in his pocket, to be exact. I know that for a fact. I have a letter from him so informing me. He felt that at any time a major emergency might develop. Moreover, on Thursday, he drew out an additional five thousand dollars from his account. He planned to attend an auction sale of rare books on Friday afternoon."

"Well?"

"When I arrived here to take charge, I was given the things that were on his body at the time of death—the clothes and personal possessions, watch, cardcase, and— the wallet."

"What about the wallet?" Bertha Cool asked, her eyes glittering with eagerness.

"In the wallet," Christopher Milbers said, "there was one one-hundred-dollar bill, one twenty-dollar bill, and three one-dollar bills—nothing else."

"Oh, *oh!*" Bertha Cool observed.

"You can imagine my perturbation."

"Did you say anything?"

"Well, a person dislikes to say anything which might be considered an accusation until he is certain of his ground."

"So you want me to make you certain of your ground, is that it?"

"Well, not exactly that. I'm certain now."

"Yes?"

"Yes. Miss Dell, you know."

"What about her?"

"She knows about the money being in his possession."

"How come?" Bertha asked.

"Miss Dell was his secretary for more than a year, and she remembers the occasion when he dictated the letter in which he said he was going to keep five thousand dollars on hand. That is, she did after I refreshed her memory."

"Where is the letter?" Bertha asked.

"I have it in Vermont—that is, I hope I have it there. I very seldom destroy important correspondence."

"Correspondence from your cousin was considered important?"

"Frankly, Mrs. Cool, it was."

"Why?"

"He was my only living relative. I felt very close to him, very much attached to him. You know how it is when the family circle narrows down to just two people." Milbers beamed at her over his finger tips.

"And one of them is wealthy," Bertha Cool supplemented acidly.

Milbers didn't say anything.

"How long since you'd seen him?" Bertha asked.

"It had been some time—four or five years."

"You didn't keep up with him very well, considering

all the facts."

"He preferred it that way. He liked to write, but as far as personal contact was concerned—well, I thought it was better in the interests of a harmonious family relationship to let our contact be by correspondence."

Bertha said, "That's one of those pretty speeches that sound as smooth as silk until you stop to pick the words to pieces to see what they mean. I'd say that you didn't get along too well."

"In oral conversation," Milbers admitted, choosing his words with careful precision, "we had our differences. They were predicated upon certain radical political and economic beliefs. In carrying on a correspondence, it is possible to avoid certain controversial subjects if one is tactful. In a conversation, it is not so easy."

Bertha said, "You could save a lot of your time and a lot of mine if you'd come right out and call a spade a spade."

Milbers's eyes lit up with the fire of enthusiasm. "Ah, Mrs. Cool, there you go, making exactly the same error that so many people make. A spade is *not* a spade. That is, a spade is a very rough general classification covering gardening implements of a certain conventionalized shape but used for different purposes. There are spades and shovels. There are various types of spades and various types of shovels. Popularly, a shovel is considered a spade, and a spade considered a shovel. As a matter of fact, however—"

"Skip it," Bertha said. "I can appreciate why your cousin felt the way he did. Go on from there."

"You mean about the spades?"

"No, about your cousin. Where did he live? Hotel, boarding-house, club, or—"

"No, Mrs. Cool. He didn't live in any of those places. Unfortunately, he sought to maintain his own domicile."

"Who ran it for him?"

"A housekeeper."

Bertha's glittering eyes commanded additional information from her visitor.

"A Mrs. Nettie Cranning. A woman who, I should say, is somewhere in the forties. She has a daughter, Eva, and a son-in-law, Paul Hanberry."

"Paul and Eva live in the house with them?" Bertha asked.

"That's right, Mrs. Cool. Paul was the chauffeur who drove my cousin around on the somewhat rare intervals when he went places in an automobile. Mrs. Cranning, Paul, and Eva Hanberry lived there in the house. Eva, I believe, acted technically as an assistant to her mother. They all drew rather large salaries, and it was, if you ask me, a highly inefficient and expensive arrangement."

"How old is Eva?"

"I should say around twenty-five."

"And her husband?"

"About ten years older."

"What do *they* say about the money that was supposed to have been in the wallet?"

"That's just the point," Milbers said. "I haven't mentioned it to them."

"Why not?"

"I am very much concerned that whatever I do say won't seem to be an accusation; yet I feel it is something that should be discussed."

"Do you, by any chance, want me to do the discussing?" Bertha asked with a sudden flash of inspiration.

"That's right, Mrs. Cool."

Bertha said, "I'm good at that."

"It's a field in which my weakness is deplorable," Milbers admitted.

Bertha, regarding him speculatively, said, "Yes, I can imagine—if the housekeeper is of a certain type."

"Exactly," Milbers agreed, separating his finger tips and bringing them together again at regular intervals. "She's precisely that type."

"Now, there was a letter about one five thousand dollars in cash. How about the other five grand?"

"That was because my cousin wished to attend an auction of some rare books. His sickness prevented him from doing so. His bank, however, confirms the five thousand withdrawal. As I compute it, Mrs. Cool, my cousin had—must have had—ten thousand dollars in his wallet at the time of his death."

Bertha puckered her lips, whistled a few bars, and asked suddenly, "How about you, are you well fixed?"

"What does that have to do with it?"

"It gives me the whole picture."

Christopher Milbers, after deliberating for a moment, said cautiously, "I have a farm in Vermont. I make maple sugar and sirup, and sell by mail. I make a living, but I can't say I do any more than that."

"Your cousin a customer?"

"Yes, he bought his sirups from me. He liked maple sugar, but had that sent to his office rather than the house. From time to time I would send him samples of new confections I was putting out—sent him one, in fact, only last week. It's so hard to think of him as not being still alive—"

"Large samples?"

"No. Definitely not. In selling sweets, one never sends enough to cloy the taste, only just enough to whet the sweet tooth."

"Charge your cousin, or send him the stuff free?"

"I charged him regular list less thirty per cent—and he always was careful to take off an additional two per cent for cash."

Bertha held up her right hand, the first and second fingers spread wide apart in a V. "In other words," she said, "you and your cousin were close to each other—just like this."

Milbers smiled. "You should have known my cousin. I doubt if anything ever got close to him—not even his undershirt."

"No? How about the housekeeper?"

A shadow crossed the man's face. "That is one of the things that worries me. She undoubtedly wanted him to become dependent upon her. I am a little afraid of her."

"I'm not," Bertha said. "Let's go."

Chapter Eight

NETTIE CRANNING, red-eyed with grief, gave Bertha Cool her hand and said, "Do come in, Mrs. Cool. You'll pardon me, but this has been a terrible shock to me—to all of us. My daughter, Eva Hanberry, and this is my son-in-law, Paul Hanberry."

Bertha invaded the reception hallway with brisk competence, shook hands with everyone, and forthwith proceeded to dominate the situation.

Nettie Cranning, a woman in the early forties who devoted a great deal of attention to her personal appearance and had cultivated a mannerism which was just short of a simper, quite evidently tried to be a perfect lady at all times.

Her daughter Eva was a remarkably good-looking brunette with long, regular features, thin, delicate nostrils, arched eyebrows, a somewhat petulant mouth, and large, long-lashed black eyes which seemed quite capable of becoming packed with emotion if occasion presented.

Paul Hanberry seemed very much a masculine nonentity, drained dry by the relatively stronger personalities of the two women. He was of average height, average weight; a man who created no particular impression. As Bertha Cool expressed it afterward in her letter to Donald Lam, "You could look at the guy twice without seeing him."

Christopher Milbers promptly effaced himself into the background, hiding behind Bertha Cool's dominant personality as though he had been a child tagging along when his mother went to school to "investigate" the administration of a discipline of which she did not approve.

Bertha lost no time getting to the point.

"All right, folks," she said. "This isn't a social visit. My client, Christopher Milbers, is getting things cleaned up here."

"Your client?" Mrs. Cranning asked with cold, arch reserve. "May I ask if you're a lawyer?"

37

"I'm not a lawyer," Bertha said promptly. "I'm a detective."

"A detective!"

"That's right."

"Well, good heavens!" Eva Hanberry exclaimed.

Her husband pushed his way forward. "What's the idea of having a detective in on the job?" he asked with a ludicrous attempt at bluster which made it seem as though he might be trying to bolster his own courage.

Bertha said, "Because there's ten thousand dollars missing."

"What?"

"You heard me."

"Are you," Mrs. Cranning asked, "accusing us of taking ten thousand dollars?"

"I'm not accusing anybody," Bertha said, then waited a moment and added significantly, "yet."

"Would you kindly explain exactly what you mean?" Eva Hanberry demanded.

Bertha said, "When Harlow Milbers died, he had ten thousand dollars in cash in his wallet."

"Who says so?" Paul Hanberry asked.

"I do," Christopher Milbers announced, coming forward a step so that he was standing at Bertha Cool's side, "and I happen to be in a position to prove my statement. My cousin was intending to negotiate for the purchase of some very rare contemporary historical books. Because of certain considerations which needn't enter into the discussion, the purchase was to be for currency. He had ten thousand dollars in currency in his possession the day he died."

"Well, he hid it somewhere, then," Mrs. Cranning said, "because it wasn't in his wallet when he died."

"No, he didn't," Christopher Milbers said. "He always kept five—"

Bertha Cool brushed him backward and into silence with a sweeping gesture of her arm. "How do you know it wasn't in his wallet when he died?" she demanded of Mrs. Cranning.

Mrs. Cranning exchanged glances with the others, and failed to answer the question.

Eva Hanberry said indignantly, "Well, good heavens, I guess if we're responsible for things here, it's up to us to look through the things a dead man leaves, isn't it?"

Paul Hanberry said, "We had to find out who his relatives were."

"As though you didn't know," Christopher Milbers said.

Bertha Cool said belligerently, "I didn't come out here to waste time in a lot of arguments. We want that ten thousand dollars."

"He *might* have concealed it in his room," Nettie Cranning said. "I'm quite certain it wasn't in his wallet."

"It most certainly wasn't in his wallet by the time *I* got it," Milbers said, growing bolder as Bertha Cool's direct tactics got the others on the defensive.

"All right," Bertha observed. "That's a starting-point. We'll go look at the room where he died. How about the other rooms? Did he do any work here in the house?"

"Good heavens, yes. Lots of it in the library," Mrs. Cranning said. "He worked there until all hours of the night."

"Well, let's take a look in the library. Which is closer?"

"The library."

"Let's go there first."

"The bedroom's been searched, anyway," Paul said. "He—"

Mrs. Cranning silenced him with a glance of savage disapproval.

Eva said in a low voice, "Let Mother do the talking, dear."

Mrs. Cranning, with considerable dignity, said, "Right this way," and led the way into a spacious library. In the doorway, she made a little sweeping gesture with her hands as though turning the room over to the visitors and, incidentally, disclaiming all responsibility for herself.

Paul Hanberry looked at his watch, suddenly jerked to

startled attention, said, "Gee, I forgot a telephone call," and walked hastily toward the back of the house.

Almost instantly the attitude of the two women changed. Mrs. Cranning said in a more conciliatory voice, "Are you *absolutely* certain that he had the money with him?"

"Probably in his wallet," Milbers said. "The banker is positive that's where he put the five thousand dollars he drew out Thursday."

Nettie Cranning and her daughter exchanged glances. Eva said defensively, "He wasn't ever alone in the room with Mr. Milbers. You know that as well as I do, Mother."

"Not *before* he died," Mrs. Cranning said, "but—"

"*Mother!*"

"Oh, all right! But you were the one who brought the matter up."

"Well, you as good as accused—"

Mrs. Cranning turned to Bertha with a smile. "Of course, Mrs. Cool, this is a great shock to us and a great surprise. We want to do everything we can to help you—if you want our help."

"Oh, certainly," Bertha said dryly. "And you'll really be surprised to find how much *I* can do."

The library was a huge room lined with shelves of books, many of them bound in a leather which had turned a dark, crusty brown with age. In the center of the room was a long table, and this table was fairly littered with books lying open, piled one on top of the other. In the center was a writing-pad and a pencil. The top page of the pad was scrawled with notes written in an angular, cramped hand.

Mrs. Cranning said, "I don't think anyone's looked through here except Mr. Christopher Milbers, who asked to look through the whole house. It's just the way poor Mr. Milbers left it. He gave orders that no one, under any circumstances, was to touch any of the books or things in this room. They were all to be kept just as he left them. Sometimes there would be days on end when

I couldn't get at the table to dust it because it was so littered with things that I couldn't touch."

"It's hardly a place where a person would leave ten one-thousand-dollar bills," Bertha observed.

Mrs. Cranning's silence showed that she felt the same way.

Christopher Milbers said, "I have already examined the notes that are on that pad of writing-paper. They have to do with one of the campaigns of Caesar. They have no bearing whatever on the subject under discussion. In fact, I found them singularly uninteresting—"

Bertha Cool moved away from him and swept through the room in a hurried search.

"I feel," Milbers said, "that we may concentrate our search in the bedroom. However, I think we are all agreed that the search is destined to be fruitless. So far as *I* am concerned, it is merely a necessary preliminary before lodging a formal charge."

"Against whom and for what?" Eva Hanberry demanded with swift acerbity.

Christopher Milbers detoured the suggestion very adroitly. "That," he said, "is entirely in the discretion of the detective."

"Just a *private* detective." Mrs. Cranning sniffed. "She has no authority to do anything."

"She is my representative," Milbers announced, managing to put great dignity into the statement.

Bertha Cool ignored this discussion. On the trail of money, she was as eager as a hound on a scent. She walked over to the library table, glanced at the open books, riffled the closely written pages of the pad, paused half-way through to read what had been written there, and said, "Who gives a damn about that old stuff?"

After a moment's silence, Christopher Milbers said defensively, "My cousin was interested in it."

"Humph!" Bertha said.

Once more there was an interval of silence.

"Any drawer in this table?" Bertha asked.

Quite apparently there was none.

"I think we may as well adjourn to the bedroom," Milbers said.

Bertha once more regarded the pad of paper with so many of the pages filled with scrawled notes.

"What becomes of this stuff?" she asked.

"You mean the notes?" Mrs. Cranning asked.

"Yes."

"They were given to his secretary to be transcribed; then Mr. Milbers would read them and correct them for final revision. After that, they'd go into his notebook. He had dozens of notebooks filled with data, and when he'd get—"

"How about these pads?" Bertha asked. "The way he wrote, a pad didn't last him very long."

"I'll say it didn't. Sometimes I've seen—"

"Where'd he get the extras from?"

Mrs. Cranning indicated a paneled bookcase. "Supplies are in there. He always kept a sheaf of pencils properly sharpened, a whole stack of these writing-pads, and extra—"

Bertha brushed past her and walked over to the cabinet. She jerked open the door, looked at the orderly rows of stationery and supplies, then turned suddenly to Mrs. Cranning and said, "What makes you think Paul took it?"

"Took what?"

"Took the ten thousand dollars."

"Why, I never thought any such thing, Mrs. Cool. You're positively insulting. I don't think you realize that Paul is my son-in-law and a very dutiful—"

"Does he play the races?" Bertha asked.

The quick glance of dismay which passed between mother and daughter was all the answer Bertha needed.

"Humph!" Bertha said. "Thought so. Probably telephoning in to his bookie right now. I'm going to tell you something. If he means anything to you, you'd better get the truth out of him. If he took it, he's probably still got most of it left."

Paul Hanberry came into the room just in time to

catch the last couple of words. "Who," he asked, "has got what left?"

"Nothing, dear, nothing," Eva Hanberry said with such perturbed haste that it was quite obvious she had a guilty desire to change the trend of conversation.

Hanberry's face flushed. "Listen," he said, "don't think you can make *me* the fall guy in this thing. I've known for a long time that I was just a supernumerary. You two women are just too damn sweet for words. Hell, you should have married each other! I don't suppose it's ever occurred to you, Eva, that when a girl grows up and gets married, she's supposed to—"

"Paul!" Eva said sharply.

Mrs. Cranning cooed sweetly, "This is neither the time nor the place, Paul, for you and Eva to air any domestic differences."

Eva Hanberry endeavored to divert attention by making a sudden frantic search of the cupboard. "After all, he might have left it in here," she said, her words having the expressionless rapidity of the patter employed by a sleight-of-hand performer in attempting to cover up some bit of trickery. "After all, he was in this room a lot, and it's quite possible that—"

"If you don't mind," Milbers said, pushing forward assertively, "*I'll* do the looking."

Bertha paid no attention to him. Her broad, capable shoulders blocked the entrance of the storage space as she started shoveling out the pile of stationery.

"Here's a drawer back here," she said.

"Of course, he couldn't have got to that with all the pads of paper in the way," Milbers observed. "Still—"

Bertha opened the drawer.

The others pushed forward. "Anything in there?" Milbers asked.

"Some pen points, stamps, and a sealed envelope," Bertha said. "Let's see what this is. The envelope looks promising."

She opened the envelope pulled out an oblong of folded paper.

"Well, what is it?" Mrs. Cranning asked as Bertha Cool's silent interest in the paper gave evidence of its importance.

Bertha Cool said, "I have in my hand a document dated the twenty-fifth day of January, 1942, and purporting to be the last will and testament of Harlow Milbers. Any of you folks know anything about this?"

"A will!" Christopher exclaimed, pushing forward.

Paul Hanberry said, "Wait a minute. What date did you say that was, January twenty-fifth? Why, I'll bet that's—"

"Bet it's what, Paul?" his wife asked as he quit speaking abruptly as though wondering whether he should continue.

"The paper he had me sign as a witness." Paul said. "Don't you remember? I told you about that Sunday when Josephine Dell was out here. He called us both into the room and said he wanted to sign something and wanted us to witness his signature. He signed in pen and ink, and then turned over a page and had us sign as witnesses."

Bertha Cool turned over the first page of the document, inspected the signatures on the second page, and said, "That's right. Two people have signed as witnesses: Josephine Dell and Paul Hanberry."

"Then that was it. That was his will."

"Why didn't you tell me?" Mrs. Cranning asked sharply.

"I told Eva he had us sign something in here. *I* thought he said it was a will."

"I never thought it really was a will," Eva said hastily to her mother. "To tell you the truth, I didn't think much of it. I remember Paul was out washing the car, and Mr. Milbers tapped on the window and asked him to come in and—"

"What's in that will?" Christopher Milbers demanded sharply. "What does it say?"

Bertha, who had been reading the document, looked over at Milbers and said, "You aren't going to like this."

"Well, come on," Paul Hanberry said, somewhat impatiently. "What's it all about?"

Bertha Cool started reading the will:

"Know all men by these presents that I, Harlow Milbers, of the age of sixty-eight years, being of sound and disposing mind and memory, and being utterly weary, not of life (for I like that) but of the people who insist on living it at the same time I do, make this my last will and testament, in words and figures as follows:

"I have only one living relative, Christopher Milbers, a cousin, a damned hair-splitting hypocrite. I have nothing in particular against Christopher Milbers except that I don't like him, that his personality irritates me, that he says too much about too little too often, and suppresses his own opinion upon controversial subjects because he hopes thereby to receive a measure of my bounty when I am dead.

"Much of the distaste with which I regard a final dissolution is due to a contemplation of the ghoulish glee with which my polysyllabic relative will prate about the sanctity of family, the true bond of relationship, and the inscrutable ways of Providence, all the while gleefully contemplating the material advantages which will ensue to him with the probating of my will.

"Taking all of these things into consideration and realizing the necessity of making some provision for my beloved cousin, in order to conform to the conventions and not to disappoint said beloved cousin too greatly, because, after all, he has taken time to write me long, uninteresting letters, I therefore give, devise, and bequeath to my said cousin, Christopher Milbers, the sum of ten thousand dollars ($10,000.00)."

Bertha turned the page. Before starting to read the second page, she surveyed the startled faces of the people about her.

"You asked for this," she said to Christopher Milbers.

Milbers, white-lipped with indignation, said, "It is an outrage—the last word of a man who has placed himself beyond reach of a reply. It was unkind. It was cowardly, but, of course—"

Bertha Cool finished his sentence for him as he became thoughtfully silent. "But, of course, ten thousand bucks is ten thousand bucks," she said.

Christopher Milbers flushed. "A mere bagatelle for a man of his means," he said. "It is definitely insulting."

Bertha Cool started reading once more from the will.

"*To my secretary, Josephine Dell, ten thousand dollars ($10,000.00).*

"*To Nettie Cranning, my housekeeper, Eva Hanberry, her daughter, Paul Hanberry, her son-in-law, all the rest of everything I own.*

"*I don't want Christopher Milbers to have anything to do with the business in court. Nettie Cranning is to be executor of my whole estate.*

"*In witness whereof, and in a slightly whimsical mood, as though this preparation for the post-mortem distribution of my property had already freed me somewhat from the burden of earthly hypocrisies, I have hereunto set my hand and seal this twenty-fifth day of January, nineteen hundred and forty-two, subscribing the document in the presence of the two persons whom I have called in to witness my signature and make it legal, declaring to them that it is my will, yet making certain they are unfamiliar with the contents thereof.*

(signed) Harlow Milbers.

"And," Bertha Cool went on, "there's an attestation clause for the witnesses following just below. I guess I may as well read it.

"*The foregoing instrument consisting of one page beside this was executed in our presence and in the presence of each of us on the twenty-fifth day of January, nineteen hundred and forty-two by Harlow Milbers, who then and there declared it to be his last will and testament, and requested us to sign as witnesses, which we did in his presence and in the presence of each other, all on this twenty-fifth day of January, nineteen hundred and forty-two. (signed) Josephine Dell, (signed) Paul Hanberry.*"

Paul Hanberry was the first to break the silence. "Jumpin' geewhillikins," he said. "The old man left his property to *us!* Why, when he asked me to sign that as a witness, I had no more idea what was in that will—I supposed, of course, it left everything to his cousin."

"You remember the occasion of signing the will as witness?" Bertha asked him.

He looked at her as though she might have been completely crazy, "Why, of course," he said. "I remember that. I'd forgotten about the will part of it. It was here in the library on a Sunday afternoon. He'd had Josephine Dell out to the house here, taking some dictation, and I was washing the car out in the driveway under the window. She came to the window and beckoned for me to come in. When I got in, the boss was sitting there at the table, holding a pen. He said, 'Paul, I'm going to sign my will. I want you and Josephine to sign as witnesses, and I want you to remember, in case anyone asks you, that I didn't seem any more crazy than usual'—or something like that. Anyway, that was the general effect of it."

Christopher Milbers said, "This is, of course, very much in the nature of a shock to me. I can hardly imagine Harlow, my beloved cousin, adopting such an attitude. However, the fact remains that we are at present engaged in searching for ten thousand dollars which seems to have mysteriously disappeared under circumstances which, at least, point the finger of suspicion—"

"Wait a minute," Nettie Cranning said suddenly. "We don't have to take that from you."

Christopher Milbers smiled, the superior smirking smile of one who takes pride in a mental agility which has trapped some fellow mortal. "I have not made any specific accusation, Mrs. Cranning. The fact that you seem to resent my comments indicates that at least in your own mind—"

He was interrupted by the ringing of the doorbell.

"See who that is," Mrs. Cranning said to her daughter.

Eva went quickly to the front door.

Christopher Milbers said, "I simply can't believe it. It's unfair. It's unjust."

"Oh, forget it," Mrs. Cranning said. "You've got ten thousand bucks, and if you think *that's* hay, you're a horse."

Paul laughed uproariously.

Bertha Cool said, "We're still ten thousand dollars short."

Voices sounded in the hall. Eva Hanberry came back into the room with Josephine Dell.

"Hello, folks," Josephine called. "What do you think? I've got the *swellest* job. I'm going to work with a man who is employed by the government. He flies all over the country, and I'm going to do a lot of traveling myself. Some kind of labor investigations. He goes to one place, stays there for a month or six weeks, and then goes to some other place. Isn't that just too grand for anything?"

Nettie Cranning said, "Wait until you've heard *all* the news."

"Yes," Eva said. "You've got some money I'll bet you didn't know anything about."

"What?"

"It's a fact," Paul assured her. "Remember that time when the boss had us witness a will?"

"Oh, you mean the time when you were washing the car and I tapped on the window and called you in?"

"Yes."

"That's right, it was a will, wasn't it? I think that's what he said it was."

"I'll tell the world it was a will. You got ten thousand dollars in it."

"I got *what?*" Josephine exclaimed incredulously.

"Ten thousand dollars," Paul said.

Bertha Cool pushed the attestation clause of the will under her nose. "Is that your signature?" she asked.

"Why, yes, of course."

"And that's the will that you witnessed?"

"Yes."

Milbers said, "We'll discuss that in greater detail later

on, but, in the meantime, I'm looking for the ten thousand dollars which my cousin had at the time of his death. I want to know what's become of it."

"Say, wait a minute," Paul said with a cunning gleam in his eyes. "*You* want to know what's become of it. Where do you get that noise? You're talking as though you had some interest in that ten thousand dollars."

"Well, I certainly have," Christopher Milbers said. "I'm his cousin."

"Cousin, hell! You get ten thousand bucks under the will, and that's all. *We're* the ones that are entitled to that ten thousand dollars. We're the ones that should get all worked up about it. It's no put-in of *yours* what happens to it, and don't forget the fact that Mrs. Cranning is the executor of the estate. I guess we're going to quit tearing the house upside down looking for ten thousand smackers that you insinuate we've stolen right now. We'll make an inventory of things in an orderly way. If we find the ten grand, we've found it. If we don't, it's our loss, not yours."

Christopher Milbers stood looking at them, swiveling his eyes from one to the other, an expression of growing dismay on his face.

"I guess you and your detective, Mrs. Cool, are all done here," Paul went on. "All washed up."

"Paul," Mrs. Cranning said, "you don't need to be crude about it. However, as far as that's concerned, Mr. Milbers has heard the will read and it was very clear. *I'm* in charge."

"That will," Christopher Milbers declared, "is illegal. It was made under undue influence."

Paul Hanberry laughed, a mocking, taunting laugh. "Try proving *that*."

"Then it's a forgery."

Mrs. Cranning said, "Be careful what you say, Mr. Milbers."

Josephine Dell said, "I'm sorry, Mr. Milbers. I don't know what's in the will, but, as far as the will itself is concerned, it's *absolutely* genuine. I remember Mr. Milbers calling us in that day in January. Paul was washing the car outside the library. Remember, Paul? You'd backed it out in the driveway. It was right under the library window, and we could hear the hose running. Mr. Milbers went over to the safe and took out this paper. He told me that he wanted to sign a will and wanted me to be one witness, and said I'd better get one of the others as an additional witness. I asked him which one, and he said it didn't make any difference. Then he said, 'Isn't that Paul washing the car out there?' and I said, 'Yes,' and he said, 'Well, tap on the window and motion for him to come in.'"

"That's right," Paul said. "And when I came in the boss said he wanted to make a will, and wanted me to sign as a witness. I didn't pay very much attention to it, because I thought—well, you know, I didn't think there was a dime in it for me."

Josephine said, "I remember you were working on the car, because there was a little grease on your right hand. You got it on the paper, and Mr. Milbers—"

Christopher Milbers grabbed at the will. "Well, there's no grease mark here" he said.

Mrs. Cranning looked over his shoulder. For a moment, she was silent with dismay.

Eva Hanberry said, "Well, a grease spot doesn't make a will; and besides, your recollection might be at fault, Josephine."

"No," Josephine Dell said firmly. "I don't care what difference it makes or who gets hurt, I'm going to tell the truth. There was a grease spot. If that grease spot isn't on the paper, it isn't genuine. Let me see my signature again."

"Wait a minute," Nettie Cranning said. "The grease would have been wiped off."

"No," Josephine said. "*I* wiped it off right away with a Kleenex I took from my purse, but it left a spot and—"

"Hold it up to the light," Nettie Cranning said. "That's the way to tell. The grease would have soaked into the paper by this time."

Bertha Cool turned back the blue backing on the will, held the second page up to the light. The oil had soaked through in a spot about the size of a dime.

Josephine Dell said, "Well, I feel better about it now, because I distinctly remembered that grease spot."

Bertha Cool said, "Now, *I'm* going to say something. I'm going to have a photographer come out here and make a photograph of this will while everybody's here. I think we're entitled to that much."

"Personally," Mrs. Cranning said, with the suddenly assumed dignity of a woman who has inherited wealth and is making a painfully conscious effort to be a lady, "I think that is a very admirable suggestion, most compatible."

"You mean commendable, Mother," Eva said.

Mrs. Cranning drew herself up to her full dignity as a woman of wealth. "I said compatible, Eva, dear."

Bertha Cool started dialing a number.

While she was waiting she said, "Subscribing witnesses can't take under a will, Mrs. Cranning."

Nettie Cranning drew herself up. "We're not going to be narrow minded about this. Eva, Paul and I get everything that's left, and we'll divide it up just the way Harlow Milbers wanted it in his will. *We're* not going to split hairs over a lot of legal technicalities. We loved Harlow Milbers and we're going to see that his wishes are carried out to the letter—aren't we, Eva?"

"Yes, Mother."

Chapter Nine

BERTHA COOL, marching into the office, paused for a word with Elsie Brand. "Of all the rotten breaks."

"Do you want to tell me about it?" Elsie Brand asked, pushing her chair away from the desk.

"No," Bertha said. "I don't want to tell anybody about it. I'm a sucker. I'm mixed up in a case where it's raining gold, and I'm caught out with a leaky teaspoon. Everybody's in the dough except Bertha! How I miss that little runt! If he were only here, he'd find some way of climbing aboard the gravy train, and we'd come out of it with some dough."

"There's a card from him in the mail," Elsie said. "He's in San Francisco, and will be there for three or four days."

"You mean Donald Lam's in San Francisco?"

"Yes."

"I'm going to fly up to see him."

"It wouldn't do any good," Elsie Brand said. "He says in his card that you can't see him, but he can get mail."

The angle of Bertha Cool's jaw showed sudden irrevocable decision. "All right, then," she said. "I'm going to write to the little shrimp. Brainy little bastard! He'll know what to do. Suppose he'll be snooty about it. He's got to tell me what to do. Bring your notebook, Elsie. I'm going to write Donald Lam every single thing that's happened."

Bertha Cool led the way into the inner office. She seated herself in the swivel chair and said to Elsie Brand, "This letter goes air mail, special delivery. Put *rush* on the envelope, *urgent, personal,* and *very private.*"

Elsie Brand's pencil moved over the paper.

"We'll start it this way," Bertha said. "Dear Donald: It was so good to hear from you, and I miss you so much. Bertha is trying to carry on the business the best she can so that you'll have something to come back to when the war is over— Wait a minute, Elsie. I guess I won't say that."

Elsie Brand looked up.

"Might give him some legal hold on me," Bertha Cool said.

"Don't you want him back in the business?" Elsie asked.

"How the hell do I know?" Bertha said irritably. "The end of the war may be a long way off. You strike that out and write this to him. Donald, darling: Since you left Bertha in the lurch, you've got to help her get things cleaned up— No, that sounds too damn much as though

I needed him. Strike that out, Elsie."

Bertha Cool was thoughtfully silent for a moment.

Abruptly she said, "We'll write it this way. Dear Donald: Bertha is quite busy this afternoon, but she's taking time out, just the same, to write you a long letter to cheer you up, because Bertha knows how it is with persons who are in the armed forces. They get lonely for letters from people who love them— Now, Elsie, you can make a paragraph there, and then go on. There isn't very much to tell you about except what's going on in the business, but because you must miss having problems to which you can turn your mind, I'm going to tell you all about a very interesting case that's in the office now."

Bertha paused long enough to think that over, then smiled beaming satisfaction. "That's the angle," she said to Elsie Brand. "That gives me an opportunity to tell him all about it without putting myself under any obligations to him, and he'll make some suggestions. You can bet on that."

"Suppose he doesn't?" Elsie Brand asked.

"Well, I'll put right in the letter," Bertha said, "that he should wire me any ideas he may have. Of course, I won't use exactly those words. I'll tell him that if he wants me to keep him posted on what's happening in the case so he'll have something to think about, he can send me a wire, giving me his ideas, and I'll write him again and let him know about developments."

Elsie Brand looked at her wrist watch. "If the letter is going to be long," she said, "perhaps you'd better dictate it directly to the typewriter if you want it to get into the mail this evening."

"Want it to get in the mail!" Bertha Cool exclaimed. "I'd send the damn thing by wire if it didn't cost too much. All right, Elsie, let's go out to your typewriter. And here's a Photostat of the will which I'm going to include in the letter, too. I got three extra copies for the office."

Chapter Ten

THE TALL, well-dressed man who spoke in the quietly modulated tones of a college graduate approached Elsie Brand's desk.

The briefcase which he carried in his right hand was a creation of heavy black leather and gleaming brass. The hand which rested lightly upon the corner of Elsie Brand's desk was soft, well-kept, the nails neatly manicured and highly polished.

"Mrs. Cool?" he inquired with just the right rising inflection of culture.

"She isn't in yet."

The man looked at his wrist watch as though not so much interested in verifying the time for himself as in conveying a subtle rebuke to Bertha Cool's tardiness. "It's nine-fifteen," he said.

"Sometimes she doesn't get in before ten or ten-thirty," Elsie Brand told him.

"Indeed?"

As no reply was made to that comment, the man went on. "I'm from the Intermutual Indemnity Company. Mrs. Cool is, I believe, the one who placed the ad in the paper asking for information about witnesses to a certain automobile accident."

Elsie met his eyes and said, "I couldn't tell you."

"You mean you don't know?" he asked in well-bred surprise.

"I mean, I couldn't tell you. I'm here to do the typing. Mrs. Cool has charge of the department that gives out information. I—"

The door pushed open.

Bertha Cool, barging into the room, said, "Did you hear anything from Donald, Elsie?" before her eyes had become sufficiently focused on the interior of the office to see the visitor.

"Nothing yet." Elsie Brand said.

The tall man moved toward Bertha Cool. "Mrs. Ber-

54

tha Cool, I take it."

Bertha, chunky and capable, looked up at the languid humor in the tall man's eyes and said, "All right, go ahead and take it."

The tall man flushed. "I didn't mean it that way, Mrs. Cool. I was merely using a colloquial expression. I'm from the Intermutual Indemnity Company."

"What's your name?" Bertha asked.

"Mr. P. L. Fosdick," he said, rolling the name over his tongue as though he were reciting something very pleasant. His well-manicured hand went to his vest pocket, producing a cardcase which snapped open and automatically extended a card. Bowing slightly, Fosdick handed this card to Bertha Cool.

Bertha took the card, looked at it, rubbed her thumbnail over the embossed lettering in a gesture of quick, financial appraisal, and said, "All right, what do *you* want?"

Fosdick said, "You have been investigating an accident case, Mrs. Cool, advertising for witnesses, in fact. My company naturally views this activity with some concern."

"Why?"

"It looks as though you were preparing to file a suit."

"Well?" Bertha demanded belligerently, her square-toed personality bristling at the suave, patronizing splendor of the tall man's manner. "What's wrong with that? I've got a right to file suit if I want to, haven't I?"

"Yes, yes, Mrs. Cool. Please don't misunderstand me. It may not be necessary."

Bertha stubbornly refused to invite him into her private office. She stood there sizing him up with greedy, glittering eyes.

The door from the corridor opened and closed. Elsie Brand coughed significantly.

Bertha didn't turn around immediately.

Fosdick said in the manner of a man attempting to be deliberately impressive. "It might not be at all necessary to file suit, Mrs. Cool. It is quite possible that the Intermutual Indemnity Company, which insures the driver of the car involved, would accept the responsibility, admit liability, and make an adequate settlement."

Elsie Brand coughed again. When Bertha didn't turn around. Elsie said, "Mrs. Cool is busy at present. Could you come back a little later?" The tone of Elsie Brand's voice made Bertha whirl.

The droopy individual who had answered her ad as one of the witnesses and who had consistently refused to give his name was drinking in the situation.

Bertha said to Fosdick, "Come in my office," and to the witness, "I'm afraid there's nothing I can do for you today."

"I'll wait, anyway," he said, smiling, and making himself comfortable in one of the chairs.

"I'm not going to have anything for you."

"It's all right. I'll wait."

"I am definitely not interested."

"All right, Mrs. Cool. All right, all right." He picked up a magazine from the table, opened it at random, and apparently became instantly interested in the printed page.

Fosdick gallantly moved over to open the door of Bertha Cool's private office, and then, bowing with well-mannered politeness, stood to one side.

Bertha, sailing on into the inner office, watched Fosdick close the door and stand by the big chair at the window, quite ostentatiously waiting for Bertha Cool to seat herself.

Sheer irritation caused Bertha to keep him standing for several unnecessary seconds before she adjusted herself in the depths of the swivel chair.

"You'll understand, of course," Fosdick went on smoothly, "that the Intermutual Indemnity Company is not *admitting* any liability. We are only engaging in a preliminary discussion looking toward a compromise of an outstanding claim, and, as I suppose you realize, there are Supreme Court decisions to the effect that any statement made under such circumstances is not admissible in evidence—since it is the policy of the law to encourage settlements wherever possible."

Bertha didn't say anything.

"Now," Fosdick went on as smoothly as flowing sirup, "we try to be just, Mrs. Cool. Many people think an insurance company is a heartless, soulless corporation intent only upon collecting as large premiums as possible on the one hand and paying out as small losses as possible on the other. The Intermutual Indemnity Company always endeavors to be fair. When our client is responsible, we make every effort to bring about a fair settlement, regardless of the financial expenditure."

Fosdick elevated the briefcase to his lap, opened it, took out a file of papers, and let Bertha Cool see varying expressions on his face as his well-manicured fingers turned over the leaves; the raised eyebrow of interest, the little *moue* of skeptical surprise, the sympathetic frown of one who is horrified at physical suffering.

Bertha said impatiently, "Okay, go ahead and say it."

Fosdick looked up. "Mrs. Cool," he said, "if you secure a proper release, duly signed by the person injured, the insurance company would be willing to pay one thousand dollars *cold—hard—cash.*"

"You're so *good* to me," Bertha said sarcastically.

"Of course," Fosdick went on tentatively, "it appears that there were no serious injuries. It is further apparent that the person you represent must have been crossing the street without proper regard for the conditions of traffic. It is indeed quite possible that she was crosssing against a red light. In court, a defense of contributory negligence would be raised, and, quite probably, sustained. However, it is always the policy of the Intermutual Indemnity Company to give the benefit of the doubt to any person who has actually been struck by a car operated by one of our insured up to and until the time such person files suit. After suit is filed, we are as adamant. We seldom lose a law suit. Once in court, we ask no quarter, and we give none. Under those circumstances, Mrs. Cool, regardless of the fact that the damage seems to have been so purely nominal, the insurance company will make you that as an offer—*one thousand dollars in cold, hard cash.*"

Fosdick closed the file of papers, carefully replaced it in the briefcase, snapped the catch on the briefcase, inserted the leather straps through the brass buckles, adjusting them carefully into position, and got to his feet. His manner was that of one who has made a very handsome gesture indeed and expects to be applauded.

Bertha Cool said, "A thousand dollars is nothing for what this woman suffered."

"A thousand dollars," Fosdick proclaimed, "is a *very* generous compromise offer."

He bowed to Bertha Cool, opened the door, started across the outer office, paused halfway to the door, and said, "It is not only our first offer but our last. The Intermutual Indemnity Company will not increase it by one red cent."

Bertha's irritation snapped the bonds of self-restraint. She shouted at him, "All right, make any offer you damn please—but you don't need to be so damned erudite about it!"

She jerked the door of her private office shut, stamped back to the swivel chair, then suddenly thought of the other visitor in the outer office. She got up, walked back to the door, and jerked it open just in time to see the door of the outer office close.

"Where's Droopy Lids?" she asked Elsie Brand, motioning toward the chair where the lackadaisical young man had been seated.

Elsie Brand said, "He got up right after the insurance adjuster went out and followed him down the hall."

Bertha's face darkened as the full significance of this move dawned upon her. "Why, damn his dehydrated soul," she said with fervor. "The two-time, chiseling, double-crossing crook—well, I'll just fix him. I'll beat it down to Josephine Dell and get her lined up before that buttinsky can chisel in on the job."

Bertha grabbed up her hat, clapped it firmly on her

silver-gray hair, and was just starting for the door when it opened. A uniformed messenger stood in the doorway with a fat envelope. "Telegram for Bertha Cool," he said, "sent collect."

"Who's it from?" Bertha Cool asked.

The messenger looked at the memorandum. "From Donald Lam, and it was sent from San Francisco," he said.

Bertha snatched at the envelope, jerked her head toward Elsie Brand, and said to the messenger boy, "Collect from her. Give him the money out of the petty cash drawer, Elsie."

Bertha Cool flounced back to her inside office and ripped open the still moist seal of the envelope. She took out a folded message which read:

LETTER RECEIVED ALSO PHOTOSTAT OF WILL CALL YOUR ATTENTION TO MARKED CHANGE IN LITERARY STYLE BETWEEN CERTAIN PORTIONS OF WILL. FIRST PAGE INDICATES DISTINCTIVE EXPRESSION OF POSITIVE INDIVIDUAL. SECOND PAGE CONTAINS SOME MATTER DOUBTLESS COPIED FROM SOME OTHER DOCUMENT, BUT LANGUAGE USED IN CONNECTION WITH BEQUESTS TO DELL, CRANNING AND HANBERRY IS FORM OF EXPRESSION SOMEWHAT ILLITERATE PERSON WOULD USE IN ATTEMPTING DISPOSE PROPERTY. ALSO ENTIRE CLAUSE ATTEMPTING NOMINATE EXECUTRIX. THESE PORTIONS INCONSISTENT WITH ARTICULATE SMOOTHNESS CHARACTERIZING EXPRESSIONS IN BALANCE OF DOCUMENT. INVESTIGATE POSSIBILITY INK ERADICATOR TO REMOVE PORTION OF WILL AND OTHER MATTER INSERTED. REGARDS AND BEST WISHES.

DONALD LAM

Bertha sat staring at the telegram, muttering under her breath, "Fry me for an oyster—the brainy little bastard!"

The door opened. Elsie Brand asked, "Is there any reply?"

"Yes," Bertha said indignantly. "Send a letter to Donald Lam at that San Francisco address. Ask him what the hell he means by putting in all those extra words about regards and best wishes when he's sending a telegram collect."

Chapter Eleven

BERTHA COOL pressed her thumb against the bell marked *Josephine Dell*, picked up the earpiece, and placed her lips near the mouthpiece of the telephone so as to be in a position to answer as soon as she heard a voice. After seconds had elapsed, Bertha pressed her thumb against the button once more. A worried look appeared on her face.

When the third pressure against the bell brought no response, Bertha rang the bell marked *Manager*.

After a few moments, a heavy-set woman whose flesh seemed to have no more consistency than jelly on a plate opened the door and smiled at Bertha. "We have some very nice vacancies," she said in a high-pitched voice as though reciting a piece she had learned by heart. "There's one very nice southern exposure, another apartment on the east. Both of these get plenty of sunlight and—"

"I don't want an apartment," Bertha Cool said. "I'm looking for Josephine Dell."

The cordiality left the manager's face as though she had reached up and lifted off a mask. "Well, there's her bell," she said irritably. "Ring it."

"I have. She isn't home."

"All right, there's nothing *I* can do about it."

She turned away.

Bertha Cool said, "Wait a minute. I'm trying to get some information about her."

"What do you want?"

"It's very important that I get in touch with her, very important indeed."

"There's nothing I can do about it."

"Can't you tell me where she is, where I could locate her, or how I could get a message to her? Hasn't she left any instruction with you at all?"

"None whatever. She has a young woman in the apartment with her, Myrna Jackson. If anyone will know where she is, it'll be Miss Jackson."

"How can I reach Miss Jackson, then?"

"She isn't in?"

"No. No one answers the bell."

"Then *she* isn't in. There's nothing I can do. Good day."

The door slammed.

Bertha scribbled a note on the back of one of her cards. *Miss Dell, call me immediately. It's very important. There's money in it for you.*

She dropped this note into the box and was turning away when a taxicab slued around the corner and came to a stop.

The nameless young man who had answered Bertha's ad calling for witnesses to the accident alighted from the cab, looked at the meter, and stood with his back to the sidewalk, making change for the cab driver.

Bertha marched purposefully toward him.

The cab driver, seeing her approach and thinking he had another fare, jumped out from behind the wheel to run around and hold the door open.

Bertha was within three feet of the passenger when he turned around and recognized her.

Bertha Cool said, with every evidence of satisfaction, "Well, that's about what I thought you'd do. It isn't going to do you any good; I got here first." There was consternation on the man's face.

"Where to?" the cabby asked.

Bertha gave him the address of her office, turned to grin triumphantly at the droopy man.

"So you beat me to it?"

"Yes."

"How much did they offer?"

"None of your business." Bertha told him.

"You got her address from me on the distinct understanding that you weren't going to represent her."

Bertha Cool said, "I can't help it if an insurance company comes in and drops things into my life."

"That isn't fair to me."

"Baloney," Bertha Cool said. "You tried to play both ends against the middle."

"I'm entitled to be in on this."

The cab driver said to Bertha, "Are you ready to start or do I charge waiting time?"

"*I'm* ready to start," Bertha said.

"Wait a minute. This is *my* cab."

"No, it isn't," Bertha told him. "You've paid it off."

"Did you see her and actually get her signed up?" the man asked.

Bertha grinned at him, a grin of complete satisfaction. Then the man suddenly hopped into the cab beside Bertha and said, "All right, I'll ride back. I want to talk with her. We'll both take the cab. Go ahead."

The cab driver slammed the door, walked around, and got in behind the wheel.

Bertha said, "I've got nothing to talk over with you."

"I think you have."

"I don't."

"You'd never have got in on this at all if it hadn't been for me."

"Baloney. I put an ad in the paper. You thought you could make something out of it. You've chiseled in all the way along the line, trying to cash in on something."

"They offered a thousand, didn't they?"

"What makes you think so?"

"From what the adjuster said."

"Oh, you followed him from my office and pumped him then?"

"I rode down in the elevator with him."

"I thought you would."

"Now, look, you can't do this to me."

"Why not?"

"You can get more than a thousand if you play it right. I'll bet you could get twenty-five hundred inside of ten days."

"A thousand suits me," Bertha said, "and suits my client. After all, a thousand berries for a headache isn't to be sneezed at."

"But she could get a lot more. I saw the whole thing."

"Whose fault was it?"

"You can't pump me on that. She's entitled to a lot more. She had a concussion."

"Who told you so?"

"Her roommate."

"Well, it's all settled now," Bertha told him, "so there's nothing for *you* to worry about."

"I ought to have something out of this, anyway. It wouldn't hurt you any to cut me in for a hundred dollars."

"Cut yourself in," Bertha told him.

"I may, at that."

Bertha said, "I'll tell you what I'll do. I'll make you exactly the same proposition I made in the first place. Twenty-five dollars and you forget the whole business and fade out of the picture."

He settled back against the cushions with a sigh. Okay," he said. "It's highway robbery, but you've made a deal."

Bertha Cool entered the office and said to Elsie Brand, "Elsie, make out a receipt for this man to sign. Twenty-five dollars in full for account of any and all claims of any sort, nature, or description covering present claims and any contingencies that may arise from future developments. Follow the form of that receipt Donald Lam made out for the man to sign in that case a couple of months back."

Elsie Brand whipped a letter out of her typewriter, jerked a sheet of paper out of the drawer in her desk, fed it into the roller, and said, "What's his name?"

"Damned if I know," Bertha said, turning to the man.

"What's your name?"

"Jerry Bollman."

Bertha Cool said, "Sit down. I'll get you the twenty-five."

Bertha went into her private office, unlocked the desk, took out the cashbox, unlocked it, took out twenty-five dollars, but waited to take it back to the outer office until her ears told her that Elsie Brand's typewriter had quit clacking. Then she came marching out, took the receipt Elsie handed her, read it, pushed it in front of Jerry Bollman, and said, "All right, sign here."

He read the receipt and said, "My God, this signs away my soul."

"More than that," Bertha told him facetiously. "Otherwise it wouldn't be worth the twenty-five bucks."

He grinned at her maliciously, saying, "You're damn smart, aren't you?" and took the fountain pen Bertha Cool extended him. He signed the receipt with a flourish, gave it to her with his left hand, and held out his right for the two tens and the five which Bertha gave him.

Bertha handed the receipt to Elsie Brand. "File this."

Bollman said, "I could go broke working for *you*."

Bertha said, "Most witnesses tell what they know just by way of being decent."

"I know," Bollman said wearily. "I got cured of that a long time ago. Well, I'll go down and buy a package of cigarettes. That and the expenses will just use up the twenty-five. Perhaps we can do business again some day."

"Perhaps," Bertha said, and watched him walk out.

"Thank God, he didn't want to shake hands," she told Elsie Brand. "Now ring up the residence of Harlow Milbers. Ask for Mrs. Nettie Cranning. Tell her Bertha Cool wants to speak with her on the telephone. Buzz my office when you get her."

Bertha went into her private office and settled down to a cigarette in her long, carved ivory holder. When the buzzer sounded, she picked up the receiver, said, "Hello," and heard Mrs. Cranning's voice saying, "Hello, Mrs. Cool."

Bertha instantly radiated cordiality. "How *do* you *do*, Mrs. Cranning? I'm very sorry I bothered you, but I wanted to get in touch with Josephine Dell right away. I thought she might be out there. I hope I haven't bothered you."

"Not at all," Mrs. Cranning said with equal cordiality. "She was here until about half an hour ago, then a man rang up and asked her to meet him. I didn't get all that it was, but it was something very important about an automobile accident."

"A man?" Bertha Cool asked.

"Yes."

Bertha Cool was frowning. "You didn't catch the name, did you?"

"Yes, I did, but I've forgotten it. I remember she wrote it down. Wait a minute— Eva, what was that name, the one who called Josephine Dell? How is that? Okay, thanks. Mrs. Cool wanted to know."

Mrs. Cranning said into the telephone, "I have that name for you, Mrs. Cool. It was Mr. Jerry Bollman. She went somewhere to meet him."

Bertha said, "Thank you," hung up the telephone, and was halfway through the outer office before she realized the futility of her errand.

"What's the matter?" Elsie Brand asked.

"The dirty, damn, double-crossing, two-timing pretzel. That guy's so crooked he could use a corkscrew for a straight edge."

"What did he do?" Elsie Brand asked.

"Do!" Bertha said, her eyes glittering cold fire. "He invested twenty-five cents in taxicab fare to hook me for twenty-five smackers. He knew where I'd be. Probably followed me. Just because I saw him getting out of the taxicab and fumbling around for the fare, I thought he was one step *behind* me. In place of that, he was two paragraphs *ahead*."

"But I don't get it," Elsie Brand said.

"Right now," Bertha Cool said, "that guy is getting Josephine Dell's signature on a dotted line that cuts himself a piece of cake to the tune of five hundred dollars. I thought I'd fooled him by pretending to be coming *out* of Josephine Dell's apartment. I pretended I had her all signed up. He knew all along she wasn't home. It was damn sharp practice—a dirty crook."

"Who's a crook?" Elsie asked.

"He is, Jerry Bollman. The son of a bitch deceived me."

Chapter Twelve

THE BLIND MAN'S sensitive ears picked Bertha Cool's steps out of a medley of other noises. He didn't turn his head toward her, but a smile softened the man's features. He said, "Hello, I was hoping you'd stop by here. Look what I have to show you."

He opened a bag and brought out a wooden music box which he wound like a little crank. He opened the cover. and, with remarkable clarity and sweetness of tone, the music box began to play "Bluebells of Scotland."

The face of the blind man was enraptured. "I told her once," he said, "that I liked these old-fashioned music boxes, and that we used to have one that played 'Bluebells of Scotland.' I'll bet this cost her something. They're not so easy to find now. not those that are in good condition. There isn't a single note missing, and I can feel how smooth the finish on the wood is. Isn't it beautiful?"

Bertha Cool agreed that it was. "Josephine Dell sent it to you?"

"Of course. A messenger brought it and said that he'd been instructed to deliver it to me from a friend. But I know who the friend is, all right. That isn't all," he said. "She sent me some flowers."

"Flowers!"

"Yes."

Bertha started to say something, then caught herself.

"I know," the blind man went on. "It's rather peculiar to send flowers to a blind man, but I can enjoy the fragrance, anyway. I think she mainly wanted me to have the note that went with them, and she thought she could send it with flowers. The music box is expensive, and she didn't want me to know she'd done that for me."

"What's the note?" Bertha asked.

"I have it here," he said, and took a folded note from his pocket. It read:

Dear Friend:

Thanks so much for thinking of me, and even going to the expense of getting Mrs. Cool to find me. I'm sending you these flowers as a little token of appreciation and of my friendship.

The note was signed *Josephine Dell.*

Abruptly Bertha Cool reached a decision. She said to the blind man, "There's one thing I want you to do for me."

"What?"

"I want you to let me have this note."

"It's rather a keepsake. I can't read it, of course, but I—"

"You can have it back," Bertha said, "within a day or two, but I want to take it."

"Oh, all right, just so you bring it back—as soon as you can, please. You could drive by the little place where I live—1672 Fairmead Avenue—if you wouldn't mind?"

"Sure thing." Bertha promised affably. "I'll get it back to you."

Bertha tucked the note into her purse and went to a handwriting expert whom she knew.

"Look." she said. "I don't want to be played for a sucker. I don't want you to take a lot of photographs and wrap your opinion up in a lot of hooey, but here's a Photostat of a will. One of the subscribing witnesses is a Josephine Dell. Here's a note actually signed by Josephine Dell. I know that's her signature. Now this signature on the will *may* be a forgery. I want to find out. And you'll notice the first part of the second page. The language seems different in some way from the rest of the will."

The handwriting expert took the Photostat and studied it closely, apparently thinking out loud as he looked at it. "H'mmmm, all in typewriting—seems to have all been done on the same typewriter, all right. Signature on the note, peculiar spacing, unusual method of making a 'D.' Same thing in the signature of the witness on the will. If it's a forgery, it's a good one. Looks okay—would much prefer to have the original will rather than this Photostat."

"I can't get the original," Bertha told him. "You'll have to work it out from this."

"All right, I'll call you up at your office and let you know. It'll be just an opinion. If I were going to have to swear to it. I—"

"I know," Bertha said. "This is just an opinion between you and me."

"That's right."

"Call me at my office within an hour."

"That's too soon."

"Call me anyway," Bertha said.

She went back to her office, and within an hour had the telephone call.

"The signatures were both written by the same person," the expert said.

Bertha Cool thought that over.

"Are you still there?" the expert asked.

"Yes."

"I didn't hear you and thought you might have hung up."

"I'm thinking," Bertha said, getting an idea. "If that will is okay, I'm out on a limb."

"It's okay," the expert said.

Bertha Cool hung up.

Bertha pressed the buzzer which summoned Elsie Brand.

"Take a letter Elsie," Bertha said. "It's going to be to Donald. I'm going to tell him every single thing that's happened. There's something completely cockeyed about this whole business. It's raining dollar bills, and, in place of being out there with a bushel basket, I've got a net deficit of twenty-five bucks."

Bertha had just finished dictating a long letter when Christopher Milbers entered the office.

"Hello," Bertha said, "come on in," and to Elsie, "Be sure we get that out tonight, Elsie. It's air mail, special delivery."

Elsie Brand nodded, sat down at the typewriter desk, flipped back the pages of her shorthand notebook, and turned the keyboard of her machine into a pneumatic riveter.

Christopher Milbers adjusted himself in the client's seat, placed his finger tips together, and beamed across at Bertha Cool. "I came in," he said, "to settle up."

"You mean you're all finished?" Bertha asked. "You've reached a compromise with them?"

He raised his eyebrows. "Compromise? On what?"

"On the will."

He said, "I haven't as yet made up my mind what to do about the will."

"Well," Bertha asked him, "why not wait until you get the thing straightened up?"

"But," Milbers expostulated, "that wouldn't affect *your* compensation in any way. I employed you to help me locate the missing ten thousand dollars. We found the will while we were searching, but that is what we might call a side issue."

"Oh, I see," Bertha said dryly.

"I believe," Milbers announced, pressing his hands so firmly together that the fingers arched backward, "you put in something less than half a day on the matter. However, I'm willing to be generous. If you don't divide your days, I'm willing to pay for a full day."

He beamed across at Bertha.

Bertha said, "A hundred dollars."

"But, my *dear* Mrs. Cool, that's definitely outrageous!"

"What makes you think so?"

"The charges made by other firms engaged in a similar line of business—and which, incidentally, determine *legally* the reasonable basic rate. I hadn't anticipated anything like that. I had thought that your charges would not exceed ten dollars, and I had prepared a little surprise for you."

69

He took from his pocket a check payable to Bertha Cool to the amount of twenty-five dollars. On the back of it had been typed: *This check is offered and accepted in full settlement of any and all claims which the payee may have against the payor of any sort, nature, or description, up to and including the date of the endorsement of this check, and the payee, by endorsement hereof, releases the payor from any and all claims of any sort, nature, or description from the beginning of the world to the date of said endorsement.*

"Done by a lawyer," Bertha grunted.

"Well," Milbers said, "naturally I had to consult an attorney to protect my interests in connection with the estate."

Bertha knew when she was licked. She sighed, took the check, and said, "All right, then, I'll deposit it."

Milbers got to his feet, bowed, and extended his hand. "It was a pleasure to have met you, Mrs. Cool."

Bertha clasped her pudgy, competent fingers around Milbers's long, tapering hand. "All right," she said, and then added grimly, "Better luck next time."

When Milbers had left the office, Bertha strode out to the outer office, and slammed the check down on Elsie Brand's desk. "Put a P.S. on that letter to Donald, Elsie. Tell him that so far I've broken even in the damn case. Twenty-five dollars paid out. Twenty-five dollars taken in. Thank God, I'm holding my own."

Chapter Thirteen

1942 AUG 29

VALLEJO, CALIFORNIA

(DAY LETTER COLLECT)

BERTHA COOL, CONFIDENTIAL INVESTIGATIONS
   DREXEL BUILDING
      LOS ANGELES, CALIFORNIA
MORE I THINK OF IT, MORE I AM IMPRESSED WITH POSSIBLE SIGNIFICANCE OF CHANGE IN LITERARY STYLE OF THAT WILL. ANOTHER THING I CAN'T UNDERSTAND IS WHY INSURANCE

COMPANY SHOULD APPROACH YOU WITH OFFER OF SETTLE-
MENT INASMUCH AS COMPANY SHOULD KNOW IDENTITY AND
LOCATION OF INJURED PARTY. AS YOU ARE NOT AN ATTOR-
NEY THERE IS NO REASON WHY INSURANCE COMPANY
SHOULDN'T HAVE APPROACHED INJURED PARTY DIRECT UN-
LESS FOR SOME REASON INSURANCE COMPANY SHOULDN'T
KNOW THE IDENTITY OF THE VICTIM. THE DRIVER OF THE
CAR SHOULD HAVE TOLD THEM THIS. IF HE DIDN'T IT INDI-
CATES SOME COMPLICATION WORTHY OF INVESTIGATION.
REGARDS.

DONALD LAM

Chapter Fourteen

BERTHA COOL stood at her desk, holding a heavy palm
down on the open telegram as though afraid that it
might get away from her. She pressed the buzzer which
summoned Elsie Brand.

"Take a letter to Donald, Elsie— Dear Donald: You've
been in the Navy so long you're full of beans. Bertha
had the best handwriting expert in the city go over that
will and compare signatures. The signatures are genuine.
It may not have occurred to you that the peculiar change
in style comes on the *second* page. That's the page that
has the signatures. Therefore, if there's anything wrong
with *that* page, the signatures must have been forged—
all three of them.

"You got that, Elsie?"

"Yes, Mrs. Cool."

"All right, now we'll give him the other barrel— Apparently your experience in the Navy has let your brains
get rusty. It doesn't make a damn bit of difference to
Bertha whether the *second* page of that will is forged or
not, and there isn't any chance it *could* have been forged.
I'll admit that Paul Hanberry looks to me like something the cat dragged in. I wouldn't trust him as far as I
could toss my income tax with my left hand, but Josephine Dell is all right. Sometime when you're out on
the ocean with nothing to think about except dive

71

bombers, torpedoes, submarines, and mines, you may realize that Bertha's client gets his slap in the face on the *first* page. It doesn't make a damn bit of difference to Bertha what happens in the rest of the will. The testator could give the rest of his dough to superannuated naval officers for all Bertha cares. If you're going to keep on wiring me collect, at least try to get something constructive into your telegrams.

"Bertha misses you, but the way you miss all the important points on a case, perhaps it's just as well if we dissolve the partnership. Thank you, however, for trying to help. Don't bother with it any more. Bertha will take care of it. You concentrate on the enemy. Best wishes."

Bretha crumpled the telegram, dropped it into a wastebasket, looked at the crumpled ball for a moment, then fished the telegram out, smoothed it out, and said to Elsie, "Put it in the file. It's the first time the little runt ever got caught off first base, and having it in writing may not hurt anything."

As an afterthought she added, "Okay, it's Saturday. We've had one hell of a week. Let's close up shop until Monday."

Chapter Fifteen

1942 AUG 30

VALLEJO, CALIFORNIA

(NIGHT LETTER COLLECT)

BERTHA COOL, CONFIDENTIAL INVESTIGATIONS
   DREXEL BUILDING
     LOS ANGELES, CALIFORNIA

YOU HAVE MISSED POINT. THE RULE WORKS BOTH WAYS. CHANGE IN STYLE ONLY INDICATES ENTIRE CONTENTS OF WILL NOT WRITTEN BY SAME PERSON. IF SECOND PAGE OF WILL IS GENUINE THEN SOMEONE HAS SUBSTITUTED FRAUDULENT FIRST PAGE. AMOUNT OF CHRISTOPHER MILBERS'S BEQUEST IS QUITE PROBABLY CHANGED. TWO POSSIBILITIES TO CONSIDER. ONE IS THAT MILBERS HIMSELF, BEING CUT OFF WITH ONE DOLLAR, FORGED FIRST PAGE TO MAKE LEGACY

TEN THOUSAND DOLLARS. SECOND ALTERNATIVE IS THAT
CHRISTOPHER MILBERS MIGHT HAVE BEEN LEFT MUCH GREAT-
ER AMOUNT THAN TEN THOUSAND DOLLARS ON FIRST PAGE,
THEREFORE SUBSTITUTION MADE BY ONE OF RESIDUARY LEGA-
TEES. IF SECOND PAGE OF WILL IS GENUINE THEN FIRST PAGE
WAS FORGED BY SOME PERSON WITH READY GIFT OF EX-
PRESSION AND FACILE LITERARY STYLE. YOUR DESCRIPTION
CHRISTOPHER MILBERS FITS THE TYPE. HAVE YOU INVESTI-
GATED CAUSE OF DEATH OF HARLOW MILBERS? ASK PERSONS IN
ATTENDANCE TO DESCRIBE SYMPTOMS. BEST WISHES FOR
YOUR SUCCESS IN SOLVING CASE.

DONALD LAM

Chapter Sixteen

WALTON A. DOOLITTLE, Attorney at Law, regarded the
Photostat Bertha Cool had handed him.

"As I understand it, Mrs. Cool, you want to know the
legal effect of a *partial* forgery."

"That's right."

Doolittle took up the first page of the will. "Let us
suppose that this is genuine," he said, "and that the
second page containing the purported signature and the
attestation clause is a forgery."

"No chance of *that*." Bertha said.

"I understand, but I am going to consider the problem
in order. Now, a will may be revoked in any one of several ways. One of these ways is by destruction of the will
on the part of the testator. But bear in mind, Mrs. Cool,
that an unauthorized destruction *by any other person*
does *not* invalidate the will. Therefore, let us assume
that the first page of this will is genuine and that the
second page is a forgery. In other words, the first page
has been taken from a genuine will, the remaining portions of which have been destroyed; and a forged and
fraudulent second page has been added."

"You're going all the way around your elbow to get to
your thumb," Bertha said. "You're taking the same thing
I told you and wrapping it up in a lot of words."

"I want to be certain that you understand the situation," Doolittle said.

"I do."

"Under those circumstances," Doolittle went on, "the will has been destroyed, but its destruction was not a revocation. Therefore, the entire contents of the will could be proved by independent, oral evidence if we could find such evidence. Now, if the first page of the will is genuine, it is the best proof of the contents of the first page of the destroyed will. We wouldn't need to care what was in the rest of the will, once we proved the first page genuine."

"In other words, Christopher Milbers gets ten grand. Is that it?"

"Exactly."

"All right, let's get to the point. Suppose the first page is a forgery and the second page is genuine. That's more apt to be the case."

"Under those circumstances, the same rule of law applies. The destruction of a portion of the will does not constitute a partial revocation. The contents of the first page of the will could then be proven by independent, oral evidence, or, as we say in the law, by parol evidence."

"And if, in the first page of that will Christopher Milbers got a hundred thousand dollars instead of ten thousand dollars, he could still collect it?"

"If he could *prove* that that was the original will."

Bertha said, "Suppose we can prove that the first page has been substituted, but can't prove what was on the original first page?"

"Under those circumstances, in my opinion, the entire will would be refused probate, inasmuch as a court would have no way on earth of knowing what percentage of the testator's property should be affected by the residuary clause. It is quite possible that the first page of the will might have contained a dozen specific bequests."

"And if the will wasn't admitted to probate?" Bertha asked.

"Then any prior will would be effective, unless it appeared that the testator had, by some positive action, endeavored to revoke that will. It is quite possible that you could get sufficient proof of a revocation without getting sufficient proof of the contents of the genuine will which he made last."

"Then what?" Bertha asked.

"Under those circumstances, inasmuch as there is no will admitted to probate, the effect would be the same as though Mr. Harlow Milbers had died intestate, except as to the ten-thousand-dollar bequest to Josephine Dell—which is the only specific bequest for a fixed amount contained on the second page."

"And Christopher would get *all* the property except that ten thousand?"

"If he is the sole surviving relative and, therefore, the only heir at law, yes."

"And Nettie Cranning, Eva Hanberry, and Paul Hanberry wouldn't get a nickel?"

"No."

"Not even if they can prove that that page of the will giving them everything is absolutely genuine?"

"That isn't the question, Mrs. Cool. By the second page of that will, they are given, not a specific amount, but each is given an undivided one-third interest in the property passing by the *residuary* clause. It isn't as though they were given, for example, ten thousand dollars apiece. They are given the *residue* of the estate. Unless the court can determine how much of the estate was specifically mentioned in other bequests on the first page, the court can't determine the intention of the testator as to the amount of the residue. The testator might have given away half a million in the first page—or only one dollar."

Bertha Cool pushed back her chair and got to her feet. "That's the law?" she asked.

"That's my opinion, or rather, it's my interpretation of the law," Doolittle said. "It's an interesting point. There could be a very nice lawsuit over it."

"Well," Bertha told him, "something may come out of this. If it does, I'll see that you get the business."

Doolittle's smile was frosty. "So many of my clients tell me that," he said, "that I have found it's better to put it the other way, Mrs. Cool. My fee for consultation will be twenty-five dollars; then if, as you surmise, anything comes of it, that twenty-five dollars will be credited on whatever additional fee is charged."

Bertha Cool sighed and opened her purse. "Everybody seems to collect money in this case except me."

Chapter Seventeen

THE 1600 BLOCK on Fairmead Avenue, the address the blind man had given Bertha, was sparsely settled, being well on the outskirts of current real-estate development.

Conditions of the dim-out made it necessary for the cab driver to grope his way, pausing frequently to consult a map which he took from his pocket.

"This should be close to it," he said. "Somewhere on the other side of the street and a little past the middle of the block."

"Let me out here," Bertha said. "I can find it better on foot than we can by prowling around?"

"But it's more convenient to look for it this way, ma'am."

"And more expensive," Bertha snapped. "Let me out."

The cab driver slid the vehicle to a stop, jumped out, and held the door open for Bertha Cool.

"Watch your step now, ma'am."

From her purse Bertha took a small flashlight which cast its beam through a deep-purple lens. "I'm all right. Be sure to wait for me," she said, switching on the flashlight. She walked down the block, peering at numbers, and found 1672 to be a typical bungalow, set well back from the road.

The walk which led to the bungalow was of cement with a little iron guide rail on the right-hand side, and the inside of this rail was worn to a polish from being rubbed with the blind man's cane as he journeyed back and forth to his little house.

Bertha climbed the two wooden steps to the front porch and pressed the bell button. She heard the sharp clatter as the bell jangled on the inside of the house. The sound was unexpectedly loud.

It was then Bertha noticed, for the first time, that the door was blocked partially open by rubber wedges which held it in such a position there was a crack eight or ten inches wide. It was, she realized, because this door was partially open that the bell in the interior of the house had sounded so loud.

Bertha stepped to the doorway, called, "Hello. Is anyone at home?" There was no answer.

Bertha kicked out one of the doorstops, groped inside for a light switch, found it, and clicked the switch on.

Nothing happened. The room remained in absolute, utter darkness.

Bertha Cool turned the dim, purple light from her flashlight toward the ceiling of the room. It showed a chandelier hanging down from the ceiling with a cluster of sockets for light globes. But there wasn't so much as a single light globe in the place.

Puzzled, Bertha swung the beam of her flashlight, and then suddenly the solution dawned upon her. A blind man had no need for electric lights.

Bertha stepped inside the house, sending the beam of her flashlight around the room. She called once, "This is Mrs. Cool. Isn't anybody home?"

She sensed motion somewhere in the darkness. A huge, formless shadow appeared on the ceiling, slid silently across it, and vanished. Bertha jumped back. Something fluttered close to her face; then, without sound, an object settled against her neck.

Bertha flung up her arm, kicked out viciously. In a rage that was born of terror, she screamed a lusty oath.

Abruptly, the thing left her. For a moment it was caught in the unreal light in her flashlight—a bat with outstretched wings, a bat which sent its shadow projected against the far wall, making the animal seem monstrously big, bizarre, and wicked.

"Pickle me for a herring!" Bertha exclaimed, and then struck viciously at the bat, which eluded her effortlessly and glided out into the darkness.

It was a full ten seconds before Bertha could get her pulse under control and start examining the front room of the house.

Satisfied that the room was empty, she turned back toward the porch, guided by the unreal, faint illumination which sprayed out from her pocket flashlight.

It was then she noticed for the first time a jet-black streak running across the floor. At first glance she thought this was merely a stain on the carpet. Then, with another pounding of her heart, she realized that it was some sort of liquid—a little pool of the liquid, then a smear, a zigzag path, another pool, a smear, a zigzag path. It was just as the nature of this sinister track dawned upon her that Bertha Cool discovered the body.

It was sprawled face down over near a window on the far side of the room. Apparently, the man had been shot while standing near the door, and had crawled a few inches at a time, and with frequent stops, trying to gather the strength which was oozing out of him even as he waited—until finally, a pause to gather strength just under the window had been long enough to let that last pool of red mark the end of the struggle with a grim period—a period which showed black as ink in the violet light thrown by Bertha Cool's spotlight.

Abruptly, the possible significance of the open door and of the silent house dawned on Bertha Cool. She recognized the distinct possibility that a murderer was concealed in one of the other rooms, hoping to avoid detection, but ready to shoot his way out should he be discovered. The place was wrapped in Stygian darkness interspersed only by such eerie illumination as came from the flashlight Bertha Cool held in her hand. And this flashlight, designed to be used during a complete blackout, cast no well-defined beam which furnished a sharp illumination. Rather, it dissolved an indeterminate area of dense darkness into a half-darkness, showing objects with sufficient clarity to enable one to avoid stumbling over them. But there was no assurance that it penetrated the shadows in which a murderer might be lurking.

Bertha Cool started with grim competency toward the door. Her foot tangled in a thin wire, jerked some object sharply, and sent it clattering. Bertha's flashlight swung down, showing a tripod with a small-gauge shotgun lashed in position, the wire running to the trigger. Bertha's march became a retreat, then a rout. The wooden porch of the building echoed to her fleeing steps, and the flashlight bobbed and weaved in her hand as she ran down the walk.

The cab driver had turned out his headlights, and Bertha knew only that the cab should be somewhere down the street. She kept looking back over her shoulder as she ran down the sidewalk.

Abruptly the parking-lights of the taxicab snapped on. The cab driver, looking at her curiously, said, "All finished?"

Bertha didn't want to talk just then. She dove into the security of the taxicab, and slammed the door. The body lurched as the driver slid in behind the wheel, started the motor, and spun the car in a U-turn.

"No, no," Bertha said.

He turned to look back at her curiously.

"There's—I must get the police."

"What's the matter?"

"A man's dead in that house."

The curiosity in the eyes of the cab driver suddenly gave place to a cold appraisal, a calculating suspicion. He looked down at the glint of metal in Bertha Cool's right hand.

Bertha nervously shoved her flashlight back into her purse. "The nearest telephone," she said, "and don't stare at me like that."

The cab went through the gears into rapid motion,

but Bertha realized that the driver kept watching her in the rearview mirror which he had surreptitiously adjusted so that it showed her every motion. When they came to a drugstore, the cab driver didn't let her go in alone to telephone, but followed her, standing at her elbow while she notified police headquarters and waiting with her until they heard the reassuring siren of the police car.

Sergeant Frank Sellers was in the car, and Bertha knew Frank Sellers slightly by previous meetings and largely by reputation. Sergeant Sellers didn't care particularly for private detectives. His entire approach to a police problem was that of frank skepticism. As a colleague had once expressed it to Bertha, "He just looks at you and chews his cigar. His eyes call you a damn liar, but he doesn't say anything. Hell's bells, he don't have to."

Sergeant Sellers seemed in no great rush to get started for the scene of the crime. He seemed more anxious to get Bertha's story down to the last detail.

"Now, let's get this straight," he said, chewing his cigar over to a corner of his mouth. "You went out there to see this blind man. That right?"

"Yes."

"You knew him?"

"Yes."

"He'd been to you and hired you to do a job?"

"Yes."

"And you'd done it?"

"Yes."

"Then what did you want to see him about?"

That question caught Bertha slightly off guard. She said, "It was another matter."

"What?"

"I wanted to check up with him on some of the angles."

"You'd already done what he hired you to?"

"Yes—in a way."

"Well, what does that mean? What *hadn't* you done?"

"I'd done everything he wanted. There was something

on which I wanted his assistance, something on which I wanted him to check up."

"I see," Sellers said with ponderous disbelief. "You wanted a blind man to help you on some of your problems, is that it?"

"I wanted to see the man," Bertha Cool said, getting back some of her customary belligerency, "and I'm *not* going to tell you what I wanted to see him about. It's an entirely different case, and I can't afford to tip my hand on it. Now, does that clear things up?"

"Very definitely," Sergeant Sellers said, as though Bertha Cool's statement made her definitely the number-one suspect in the case. "And this blind man was lying there dead, is that right?"

"Yes."

"Face down you say?"

"Yes."

"He'd been shot?"

"I think so."

"You don't know?"

"No, I didn't perform any post-mortem on the body. There was a small shotgun there. I didn't stop to examine it. I saw what the score was and got out of there."

"He'd crawled along on the carpet from the place where he was shot to the place where he'd died?"

"Yes."

"How far?"

"I don't know. Ten or fifteen feet."

"Crawling?"

"Yes."

"And died while he was crawling?"

"He may have died while he was resting," Bertha said.

"I know, but he was in a crawling position, stomach next to the carpet, is that right?"

"Yes."

"Face turned to one side or the other?"

"I don't think so. I think his face was pressed down against the floor. I saw the back of his head."

"Then how'd you know it was the blind man?"

"Why—from his build, I guess. The blind man lives there."

"You didn't turn the body over?"

"No. I didn't touch the body. I didn't touch anything. I got out of there and called you."

"All right," Sellers said, "let's go. You've got a taxicab out there?"

"Yes."

"You'd better ride with me. Knowing it's the blind man, when you admit you didn't look at the face, makes things look kinda funny."

Sergeant Sellers turned to the taxi driver. "What's your name?"

"Harry Simms."

"What do *you* know about this?"

"Nothing at all. I takes this dame out looking for the place. She has the street number, but doesn't know where it is. There's no street lights because of the dim-out. I have a map that shows me where the place should be— that is, what block. It's pretty dark, and she's got a dim-out flashlight. When we get to the block where the house is located, I tell her about where it should be. She tells me to stop, and she'll find it herself on foot. She goes ahead and is gone for—oh, I don't know—maybe five minutes, maybe ten minutes."

"You weren't charging waiting-time?"

"No. She was pretty cagey about that. I told her I'd wait up to fifteen minutes in case she wanted to go back before then. After that, I'd either charge her waiting-time or go back. We do that once in a while when we're pretty sure of a fare back to town."

Sergeant Sellers nodded. "You sat there in the car?"

"Yes."

"What did you do?"

"Just sat there and waited."

"Radio in your bus?"

"Yes."

"Was it on?"

"Yes."

"Musical program?"

"Uh huh."

"Wouldn't have heard a shot then, would you?"

The cab driver thought that over and said, "No, I don't suppose I would—not so far down the street as where she made me stop."

As the full implications of that dawned on Bertha Cool, she said, "What are you getting at? There wasn't any shot."

"How do you know?"

"I'd have heard it if there had been."

Sergeant Sellers's eyes regarded her with an appraisal in which there was no friendliness whatever. She might have been some building on which he was making a cash appraisal.

"That all you know?" he asked the cab driver.

"That's all."

"Simms, eh?"

"Yes, sir."

"Let's take a look at your license."

The cab driver showed him his license. Sergeant Sellers took the number of the cab and said, "Okay, no reason to send you back out there. That's all. You get in my car, Mrs. Cool."

The cab driver said, "The fare's one eighty-five."

"What do you mean?" Bertha Cool snorted. "It was only seventy-five cents going out there, and—"

"Waiting-time."

"I thought you weren't charging me any waiting-time."

"Not out there. I charged you waiting-time here while you were telephoning the police and waiting for the squad car."

"Well, I won't pay it," Bertha said indignantly. "The idea of charging waiting-time on anything like that—"

"What did you expect I was going to do, stick around here and keep myself out of circulation? You're the one that stopped and—"

"Give him one eighty-five," Sergeant Sellers said to Bertha Cool.

"I'll be damned if I do," Bertha blazed. She took a dollar and fifty cents from her pocket, handed it to the cab driver, and said, "Take it or leave it. It's all one with me."

The cab driver hesitated a moment, looked at the police sergeant, then took the dollar and a half. When it was safely in his pocket, he delivered his parting shot. "She was in the house quite a while, Sergeant," he said. "When she came out, she was running, but she was certainly *in* there long enough."

"Thanks," Sellers said.

Bertha glared at the cab driver as though she could have slapped his face.

"All right," Sellers said to Bertha, "let's go."

She climbed into the automobile, taking the back seat which Sellers indicated. Sellers climbed in beside her, a police chauffeur doing the driving. There was one other man in the front seat and another beside Sergeant Sellers in the rear seat. Bertha Cool knew neither of them, and Sellers made no effort to perform introductions.

The chauffeur drove with swift skill, dimming his lights, however, as he topped the rise of ground and came within the area subjected to stringent dim-out regulations on the part of cars driving toward the ocean.

"I think it's right after the next cross street," Bertha said.

The police car slowed, crawling along close to the curb until Bertha said, "This is it."

The men climbed out. Bertha said, "I don't have to go in, do I?"

"No, not now. You can wait here."

"All right, I'll wait."

Bertha opened her purse, took out her cigarette case, and asked, "Is it going to be long?"

"I can't tell you yet," Sellers said cheerfully. "I'll be seeing you."

The men went on into the house. One of them came out after a few moments to get a camera, a tripod, and some floodlights. A few minutes later and he was back again, grumbling. "Not a damn bit of current in the whole house."

"The man was blind," Bertha said. "He didn't need lights."

"Well, I need a socket to hook up my floodlights."

"Can't you use flash bulbs?"

"I've got to," the man said. "Don't like 'em—not for the kind of stuff the sergeant wants. Can't control the lighting as well as you can with floodlights. Can't take the time to arrange things and see what you're getting, and then sometimes you get reflections. Oh, well, it's all in a lifetime."

A few minutes later, Sergeant Sellers was back. "Well," he said, "let's get some particulars. What was this man's name?"

"Rodney Kosling."

"Know anything about his family?"

"No. I doubt very much if he has one. He seemed very much alone."

"Know how long he's been living here?"

"No."

"All in all, you don't know very much about him?"

"That's right."

"What did he want you to do for him? How did he happen to get in touch with you?"

"He wanted me to find someone."

"Who?"

"A person to whom he had become attached."

"Woman?"

"Yes."

"Blind?"

"No."

"Young?"

"Yes."

"Find her?"

"Yes."

"Then what?"

"I reported to him."

"Who was the woman?"

Bertha shook her head.

"Not related to him?"

"No."

"You're certain?"

"Virtually."

"Couldn't have been that she was related to him and was tangled up with some man, and Kosling wanted to do something about it?"

"No."

"You're not being a great deal of help, Mrs. Cool."

"Hell's bells," Bertha said. "I told you about finding the body, didn't I? I could have walked out and left you holding the sack."

Sellers grinned. "I'll bet you'd have done just that, too, if it hadn't been for the taxi driver. That put you in something of a spot. You knew that after the body was discovered, he'd remember having driven you out here, and give the police a good description."

Bertha Cool maintained a dignified silence.

"Ever occur to you that this fellow is a faker?" Sergeant Sellers asked.

"What do you mean?"

"That he wasn't blind at all."

"No," Bertha said. "He was blind. I know."

"How?"

"Well in the first place, some of the things he told me about people—about what he'd deduced from sounds, voices, and steps, and things of that sort. Only a blind man could have developed his faculties that way, and—well, look at the house. Not a light in it."

"Oh, so you noticed that, did you?"

"Yes."

"Try to switch on a light, did you?"

"Yes."

"Rather unusual for you to go walking into strange houses, isn't it?"

"Well, the door was open."

Sellers said. "If you're telling the truth, you can thank your lucky stars that the blind man got home first."

"What do you mean?"

"A trap gun had been arranged so that when a person entered the house, he pulled against a thin wire, and that pulled the trigger on this four-hundred-and-ten-gauge shotgun. The moral of that is not to go wandering around strange houses just because the door's open."

"Why kill a man that way?" Bertha asked.

"Probably so someone could cook up a good alibi." Bertha thought that over.

"Well," Sergeant Sellers said, "you'll have to come in and take a look at him to make an identification. How old would you say this man was?"

"Oh, fifty-five or sixty."

"He doesn't look that old to me, and his eyes look all right."

"How long's he been dead?" Bertha asked.

Sergeant Sellers looked at her and grinned. "How long ago were you out here?"

"Oh, perhaps thirty or forty minutes."

Sellers nodded. "I'd say he'd been dead just about that long."

"You mean—"

"I mean," Sellers interrupted, "that the man can't have been dead more than an hour. If you were out here forty-five minutes ago, it's very possible that he was killed just about the time you got there. Don't bother to say anything, Mrs. Cool. Just come in and look at the body."

Bertha followed him on up the walk to the house. The men apparently had completed their investigations and were sitting on a wooden bench at the far end of the porch. Bertha could make them out as a dark huddle of humanity distinguished by three glowing red spots which marked the ends of their cigarettes, spots which streaked up and down occasionally as the men removed the cigarettes from their mouths.

"Right in this way," Sergeant Sellers said, and switched on a powerful, five-cell spotlight which turned the darkness into dazzling brilliance.

"Not over there," he said, as Bertha turned. "We've

moved him. Take a look."

The body had been placed on the table, and seemed terribly inanimate as it sprawled in the immobility of death.

The beam of Sergeant Sellers's flashlight slid along the man's clothes, paused momentarily on the red-matted garments where the bullet had entered, then slid up to come to rest on the man's face.

Bertha Cool's gasp of startled surprise gave Sergeant Sellers all the cue he needed. "It isn't Kosling?" he asked.

"No," she said.

The beam from the flashlight slid abruptly from the face of the dead man to shine full on Bertha Cool's features.

"All right," Sergeant Sellers said crisply. "Who is it?"

Bertha said dully and without thinking, "He's a dirty, two-timing chiseler by the name of Bollman. He had a good killing coming to him—and you get that damn spotlight out of my face, or I'll bust it."

Chapter Eighteen

SERGEANT SELLERS hesitated only for a moment, then said, "Pardon me," and moved the flashlight. "So this man's name is Bollman?"

"Yes."

"And how long have you known *him?*"

"About—a week or so."

"Oh, yes," Sergeant Sellers said, "and how long have you known Kosling?"

"Six or seven days."

"In other words, you've known Kosling and Bollman just about the same length of time?"

"Yes."

"This is Sunday night. Now think hard. Did you know both of them last Sunday?"

"Yes."

"What was the connection between them?"

"They didn't have any."

"But you met Bollman in connection with the matter Kosling employed you to investigate?"

"Well, only indirectly."

"And Bollman tried to chisel in on it?"

"Not on that. On something else."

"On what?"

Bertha said, "Nothing that would have anything to do with Kosling, nothing that would account for his death."

"What was it?"

"I'm not certain that I'm going to tell you."

"I think you are, Mrs. Cool. What was it?"

Bertha said, "It had to do with an automobile accident. That's something that I'm working on, and I don't think my clients would want any information made public right at the present time."

"You're not making it public. You're making it to me."

"I know, but you have a way of making reports that get into the newspapers."

"This is murder, Mrs. Cool."

"I know, but what I know about him doesn't have anything to do with his murder."

"How do you know?"

"It wasn't anything anyone would kill him about."

"But you say he's a blackmailer and a chiseler?"

"Yes."

"What makes you say that?"

"His methods."

"What's wrong with them?"

"Everything."

Sergeant Sellers said, "All right, we'll go outside and talk in the car for a little while. This is the address Rodney Kosling gave you?"

"Yes."

"Is there anything that you know that would make you think this man, Bollman, lived here?"

"No."

"You don't know where he lived?"

Bertha Cool said impatiently, "Of course not. Why ask me all that stuff? How about the man's driving-license?

89

How about his registration card? How about—"

"That," Sergeant Sellers said, "is just the point. Either someone had frisked him and taken everything that could have possibly been a means of identification, or he emptied his pockets of everything except money. Apparently his money hasn't been touched. It had evidently been taken from a wallet and pushed hurriedly down into the pockets. You wouldn't know anything about that, would you, Mrs. Cool?"

"Why should I?"

"I don't know," Sellers said. "It opens the door to some interesting speculation. The fact that the murder was committed with a trap gun indicates that the murderer wanted to claim his victim while he was far away, building up an alibi for himself. But quite evidently after the man's death, someone went through his pockets—unless the man cached the stuff from his pockets somewhere. There couldn't have been a very great margin of time, and you admit that you were here. Therefore, I ask you if you know anything about what was in his pockets?"

"No, I don't."

Sergeant Sellers said, "Well, we may as well go back to the automobile. All right, come on, boys. Charlie, you can stay here and keep an eye on the place. Usual instructions—sew it up tight. Let no one in without a pass until after the fingerprint men have finished with the place; then we'll give the newspapers a tumble and move the body. All right, Mrs. Cool, you come with us."

In the automobile Bertha Cool answered questions with monosyllables or, at times, with a tight-lipped silence. She steadfastly refused to give any information as to her connection with Jerry Bollman or the reason she had for characterizing him as a blackmailing chiseler.

Sergeant Sellers gave it up after a while. He said, "I can't *force* you to answer these questions, Mrs. Cool, but a grand jury can."

"No, they can't. I have a right to treat certain communications as confidential."

"Not the way I look at it."

Bertha Cool said, "I'm in business. I'm running a detective agency. People hire me to do things. If they wanted to tell their troubles to the law, they'd go to police headquarters in the first place."

"All right," Sellers said. "If you're thinking so much of your future business, you might remember that police good will is an asset for a private detective agency, and, on the other hand, the ill will of the police isn't going to make you any money."

"I've told you absolutely everything I know that would help clear up the case. The things I'm withholding are private matters that have absolutely nothing to do with it."

"I'd prefer to have you answer all my questions and let me be the judge of what's pertinent and relative and what isn't."

"I know," Bertha said, "but *I* prefer to handle it *my* way."

Sergeant Sellers settled himself back against the cushions. "All right," he said to the chauffeur, "we'll drive Mrs. Cool home. I'll telephone headquarters, and we'll put out a general pickup order for this blind man. Strange he isn't home. He can undoubtedly throw some light on what's happened. Let's go, Mrs. Cool."

Bertha Cool maintained an aloof, discreet silence until Sergeant Sellers had deposited her at the door of her apartment.

"Good night," he said.

"Good night," Bertha Cool announced, biting off the end of the word. She marched with unforgiving hostility across the sidewalk and up to the entrance leading to her apartment house. The police car drove away.

Almost instantly Bertha Cool left the apartment house, walked rapidly down to the drugstore at the corner, summoned a taxicab, and once she had pulled herself into the interior, said to the driver, "I want to get to the Bluebonnet Apartments out on Figueroa Street, and I haven't any time to waste."

At the Bluebonnet Apartments, Bertha Cool pushed

peremptorily at the bell button of Josephine Dell's apartment, and it was with a feeling of relief that she heard Josephine Dell's voice saying in the earpiece, "Who is it please?"

"This is Mrs. Cool."

"I'm afraid I haven't time to talk with you, Mrs. Cool. I'm packing."

"I *must* see you."

"I have this new job, and I'm packing to take a plane. I—"

"I'll talk to you while you pack," Bertha Cool said. "It will only take a few minutes, and—"

"Oh, all right." The electric buzzer released the door catch.

Bertha Cool went on up and found Josephine Dell in the midst of that seemingly hopeless confusion which comes at moving-time.

A trunk in the middle of the floor was two-thirds full. A suitcase on the bed was already filled, and there were other clothes laid out, apparently to be taken along. A small bag was on the floor by the bed, and a large pasteboard carton was about half-full of a miscellaneous assortment of odds and ends.

Josephine Dell, attired in blue silk pajamas, was literally standing in the middle of things.

"Hello," she said to Bertha Cool as though barely seeing her. "I've got all this packing to do before midnight. Going to store most of my stuff and get out of the apartment. Never realized what a hopeless job it was. Going to cram things in somehow, then take a bath, dress, and catch a midnight plane. I didn't want to be rude, but if you've ever done any moving, you know exactly how I feel."

"I know how you feel," Bertha assured her, "and I only want a minute."

She looked around for a vacant chair. Josephine Dell saw the look, laughed nervously, said, "Pardon *me*," and hurried over to lift some folded clothes from a chair by the window.

Bertha said, "I'm going to get right to the point. How would you like to receive five hundred dollars in cash?"

"I'd like it."

"I could get it for you."

"How?"

"All you need to do is to sign a release, and—"

"Oh, *that.*"

"Well, what about it?" Bertha asked.

She laughed and said, "You're the second one."

"Meaning you've already signed up?"

"No."

"Who was the first?"

"A witness who saw it. He hunted me up to tell me that it really wasn't my fault, and I could collect from the insurance company. He said he'd make a contract with me by which he'd finance the whole thing entirely at his own cost and expense, give me fifty per cent of whatever he received, and guarantee that my share would be at least five hundred dollars. I thought that was a very generous contract, don't you?"

Bertha Cool remained silent.

"But," Josephine Dell went on, "I couldn't do it. I simply couldn't. I told him I'd been thinking it over and had come to the conclusion that it was as much my fault as it was the man's who was driving the automobile— perhaps more. He tried to tell me that that didn't need to enter into it at all, that the insurance company wanted to get its files closed, and all I had to do was to co-oper- ate and take in the money just like that," and Josephine Dell gave her fingers a quick little snap.

"You wouldn't do it?"

"I just laughed at him. I told him that it was out of the question, that I'd feel as though I'd stolen the money. That man who ran into me was really very nice—and I have been out only seven dollars for a doctor's bill."

"Did you get the name of the man who was driving the car?" Bertha asked.

"No, I didn't. I didn't even take his license number. I was so rattled and shaken up at first, and then I—"

The buzzer sounded.

Josephine Dell sighed with exasperation. "I suppose," she said, controlling herself with difficulty, "that'll be someone else looking for Myrna Jackson."

"Your roommate?" Bertha Cool asked. "I'd really like to meet her."

"So would lots of people."

"Where is she?"

"Heaven knows. It wasn't a very satisfactory arrangement. She was a friend of Mr. Milbers, and he suggested we both might cut expenses by sharing this apartment. I wasn't very keen about it, but you know how it is when the boss makes a suggestion.

"Well, we tried it. She's impossible! I left a note for her yesterday saying the rent was up tomorrow, that's Monday. I told her I was going to be packing up tonight, and when she rang me up today what do you think she said?"

"What?" Bertha asked as the doorbell sounded again.

"Told me that she came up here this afternoon and had already moved out. She only moved in a short time ago, so she didn't have much stuff, but there's a five-dollar checking-out charge for cleaning the apartment, and she just didn't say a word about paying her share of that. I didn't think about it at the time."

Josephine Dell went over to the door telephone and said. "Who is it, please?" and then wearily. "No, this is her roommate. I don't know *where* she is. She left this afternoon—moved out. That's right, and I'm moving out myself. No, I *can't* see you. I can't talk with you. I'm packing. I'm undressed, and I've got to catch a midnight plane—I don't care how important it is or who you are. She isn't here. I don't know where she is, and I've done nothing all evening long but answer the doorbell for people who wanted to see her."

Josephine Dell slammed down the receiver and came back to stand in the middle of the room, looking things over with a somewhat hopeless air.

"I can't help wondering about that girl and her relationship with Mr. Milbers," she said. "Oh, it's all right as far as that end of it's concerned, but I have an idea she was snooping on me all the time she was here.

"Two weeks ago my diary disappeared. Then it showed up again, right in its accustomed place, but under some scarfs. As though I'd be sap enough to think I'd overlooked it there! She was the *only* one who could have taken it. I can imagine a girl of a certain type being interested in reading it on the sly; but why did she take it, and where did she take it?"

"Did you ask her about it?" Bertha inquired.

"No. I decided the damage had been done. I couldn't actually *prove* anything, so I decided to keep quiet and move into another apartment—a very small, cramped single. I'm fed up on this double business.

"Well," she said, changing the subject abruptly, "there's only one thing to do, and that's to get this stuff packed somehow or other. I'm sick and tired to death of trying to sort out every blessed thing I want to take. Here it goes."

She picked up bundles of folded garments and crammed them indiscriminately into the trunk and the cardboard carton.

"Can I help?" Bertha Cool asked.

"No," Josephine Dell said, and then added as an afterthought, "Thank you." Her voice and manner indicated that Bertha could be of the biggest assistance by getting out and staying out.

"What are you going to do about that will?" Bertha Cool asked. "About giving your testimony on it?"

"Oh, I'll be available when they need me," she said. "They say I may have to go down to the tropics. This is different from a week-end trip. I'm supposed to live out of a suitcase. I can't take a trunk because a lot of my travel will be on a plane. It sounded marvelous when I—"

Bertha Cool, looking Josephine Dell over thoughtfully, interrupted. "There's one thing you *can* do for me."

"What?"

She said, "I want to know something about Harlow Milbers—about how he died."

"It was very sudden, although he'd been feeling rather poorly for three or four days."

"Can you tell me something more about his exact symptoms?"

"Why, yes, of course. It started about an hour after he came to the office. He had a terrific headache, and then all of a sudden he became nauseated. I suggested he should lie down on the couch for a while, to see if that wouldn't make him feel better. I thought he went to sleep for a few minutes; then he had another spell of nausea, and that wakened him. He kept complaining of a terrific burning thirst in his mouth and throat, and I told him we should call a doctor. He said he'd go home and have the doctor come there. Then I called Doctor Clarge and told him Mr. Milbers was very ill and was taking a cab home, asking him to please go there at once to meet the cab when it arrived."

"Did you ride out with Mr. Milbers?"

"Yes."

"What happened?"

"He was sick in the cab on the way out. His stomach and intestines were terribly tender. When we got to the house, we had to help him. The cab driver was grinning. He thought the poor man had been staging a celebration."

"What did you do?"

"I helped him into the house. Mrs. Cranning came out, and she helped, too. Doctor Clarge wasn't there when we arrived, but he got there within a minute or two—before we had Mr. Milbers in bed."

"Then what?"

"The doctor stayed about half an hour and left him some medicine. He gave him a hypodermic, and Mr. Milbers felt somewhat better, although he still complained of the burning thirst and said his stomach was very sore and sensitive. He thought he was getting better, and he felt drowsy."

"Then what?"

"Doctor Clarge came back about four o'clock in the afternoon. He gave him another hypodermic, and said he thought Mr. Milbers should either have a nurse or go to the hospital that night in case he wasn't better. He left more medicine with some instructions and said he'd drop in the next morning at about eight o'clock."

"Then what?"

"About twenty minutes after Doctor Clarge had left, Mr. Milbers passed away."

"Who was in the room at the time? Were you?"

"No. Mrs. Cranning was there. I'd gone downstairs for a glass of milk and a sandwich. I'd been so upset I hadn't eaten anything. We really thought Mr. Milbers was going to get along all right."

"What happened after he died? Did you notify Doctor Clarge?"

"Yes. Doctor Clarge came out, but said there was nothing he could do. He called the undertaker, and said we should notify Christopher Milbers. I sent him the telegram."

"And then?"

"Well, what with the excitement and all of the things that had to be done, it was late when I left and then I had to go by the office to close the safe, and naturally I was pretty much upset. That's why I walked into that automobile, I guess. I don't eat breakfast, only a cup of black coffee, and that glass of milk and a sandwich was all I'd eaten all day. I hadn't even finished the sandwich because Mrs. Cranning had called me just as I was halfway through eating it."

"What did the doctor say caused his death?"

"Oh, you know how those doctors are. They roll a lot of medical terms out and look wise. Personally, I don't think Doctor Clarge knew a thing about it. I can't remember all of the words he used. I remember one of them. He said it was a gastroenteric disturbance, and that it resulted from something or other in the liver, and something or other that ended with an 'itis.' "

"Nephritis?" Bertha asked.

"I don't know. That sounds something like it. But he said the primary cause of death was a gastroenteric disturbance. I remember that much. The rest of it was a lot of mumbo jumbo about things that didn't make sense to me, and I don't think they made sense to him."

"Where did Mr. Milbers eat breakfast?" Bertha asked.

Josephine Dell looked at her in surprise. "Why, at his house, of course—that is, I suppose that's where he ate. That's why he had Nettie Cranning and Eva—and if you ask me," she blurted, "with all the service he was paying for, he should have been waited on hand and foot, in place of which he had to wait for his meals lots of times. However, it's no skin off *my* nose, and it's all over with now. But it makes me sick to think of his leaving almost everything to them."

"And ten thousand to you," Bertha Cool said.

"If he was going to leave most of his estate outside of the family," Josephine Dell said firmly, "I'm entitled to ten thousand."

"How long had you been with him?"

"Almost two years."

"That's five thousand a year."

"That's right," Josephine Dell said with sudden cold, biting rage. "That's five thousand a year. Very generous compensation, isn't it, Mrs. Cool? Well, *you* don't know everything, and don't ever kid yourself that—oh, well, what's the use? Will you please go on home now and let me finish packing?"

"That man who was a witness," Bertha Cool asked, "wasn't his name Bollman?"

"That's right. Jerry Bollman. He saw the accident, and I guess he's trying to cash in on it—seems like he does that sort of thing. Well, I've simply *got* to take some of the things out of this suitcase."

"Jerry Bollman," Bertha said, "is dead."

She picked up the top layer from the suitcase, gently placed it on the bed, said, "Well, one thing's certain. I've got to get along with only one other pair of shoes."

She took an extra pair of shoes from the suitcase, started over to the trunk, and then stopped abruptly, turned to Bertha Cool, and said, "I beg your pardon. *What* did you say?"

"Jerry Bollman's dead."

Josephine Dell smiled. "I'm afraid you're mistaken. I talked with him yesterday afternoon, and then he called again about two hours ago. Now let's see. If I put—"

"He's dead," Bertha Cool said. "He was murdered about an hour and a half ago."

"Murdered!"

"Yes."

First one shoe fell from Josephine Dell's arms; then the second one thudded to the floor. "Murdered! An hour and a half ago. How did it happen?"

"I don't know," Bertha said. "But he went out to call on your friend, the blind man. Does that mean anything to you?"

"Yes, I can understand that. I told Mr. Bollman I was afraid the light had changed just as I started across the street. He said he could get a witness to testify that he heard the noise of the accident and the sound of brakes being applied before the signal rang. I didn't realize it at the time, but I can appreciate now that the witness must have been that blind man. He's a dear—always so sweet and cheerful. I sent him a little present. You're certain Mr. Bollman was murdered?"

"Yes. He was killed when he went to call on the blind man."

"Mrs. Cool, are you *absolutely* certain?"

"Dead certain," Bertha said. "I discovered the body."

"Have they caught the man who did it?"

"Not yet."

"Do they know who did it?"

"No. They're looking for the blind man."

"Bosh!" Josephine Dell said. "He wouldn't hurt a fly! That's absolutely out of the question."

"That's what I think."

"How did you happen to discover the body?"

99

"I went out to see this blind man."

"You like him, don't you?"

"Yes."

"So do I. I think he's marvelous. I must ask him about Myrna Jackson. I saw her talking with him last week. Really, it's a crime how little I know about her. This Bollman, don't you think—I know I shouldn't say anything about him if he's dead, but—don't you think—"

Bertha said, "You're damn right I do. I don't care how dead he is. He was a heel."

"Well, heaven knows *I've* got to pack. I'm sorry, Mrs. Cool, but that's just the way I feel about that accident case, and you could stay here until midnight and not change my opinion."

Slowly, reluctantly, Bertha Cool got to her feet and headed wearily toward the door. "All right," she said. "Good night—and good luck in your new job."

"Thank you, Mrs. Cool. Good night and good luck."

"And if you don't think I could use a carload of that last, you're nuts," Bertha said with feeling, as she let herself out into the outer corridor.

Chapter Nineteen

A TAXICAB took Bertha Cool to the residence of Doctor Howard P. Rindger. Bertha rang the bell and when the doctor himself came to the door, said, "I think you remember me, Doctor. I'm—"

"Oh, yes, Mrs. Cool, the investigator. Do come in, Mrs. Cool."

"I wanted to consult you professionally, Doctor."

He looked at her shrewdly. "Feeling all right? You look as sound as a nut."

"Oh, *I'm* all right. I want to get a little professional advice."

"All right, come in this way. I have a little office fixed up here at the house for emergency treatment. Some of my patients come in at night. Now, sit down and tell me what I can do for you."

Bertha said, "I'm sorry to disturb you at this house, but it's really important."

"Quite all right. I'm always up late Sunday nights reading. Go ahead, tell me what it is."

Bertha said, "I want to find out something about poison."

"What about it?"

"Is there any poison that would take effect, say an hour or two after a breakfast at which the poison was taken, to cause nausea, a burning in the throat, and a sort of collapse that would exist until the person died?"

"When did he die?"

"Around four o'clock that afternoon."

Doctor Rindger opened the glass door of a bookcase. "Cramps in the calves of the legs?" he asked.

"I wouldn't know."

"Diarrhea?"

"Probably, but I can't tell you positively."

"Nausea persistent until the time of death?"

"At intervals, yes."

"Any treatment?"

"Hypodermics."

"Tenderness over the stomach and intestines?"

"Yes. He was very sore."

"Grayish skin? Perspiration?"

"From what was told me, I gather there might have been grayish skin."

"Anxiety? Depression?"

"I don't know."

Doctor Rindger drummed with his finger tips on the desk, reached up to the shelf, and took a book entitled *Forensic Medicine*. He opened it, and after reading a couple of pages, closed the book and put it back. "Is this just between you and me, or am I speaking officially for publication, and would I be quoted?"

"Just between you and me," Bertha told him. "You won't be quoted."

"Arsenic poisoning," he said.

"Those are the symptoms?"

"An almost typical case. The burning thirst and nausea are very typical, also the soreness over the stomach and upper abdomen. If you want to be certain, check on the diarrhea, the cramps in the calves of the legs, the feeling of depression, and note the nature of the *vomitus*. Rather a rice-water appearance in cases of arsenic poisoning."

Bertha Cool got up, then hesitated and said, "How much do I owe you?"

"That's all right—in case I'm not to be quoted or called as a witness. If I am, that, of course, will be something else."

Bertha shook hands with him and said, "I'm sorry I disturbed you this late, but it's an emergency, and I had to know tonight."

"That's quite all right. I hadn't gone to bed yet. Don't usually go to bed before midnight, although I try to finish up with my office work by eight-thirty so I have a little time to relax. How about your partner, Mrs. Cool? What's his name?"

"Donald Lam."

"That's right. Very interesting chap. Seemed to have a remarkably quick mind. I was very much interested in his reasoning on that carbon monoxide poisoning case. I knew some of the parties involved there. Some of the people were quite prominent in medical circles."

"I know," Bertha said.

"What's become of him?"

"He's in the Navy."

"That's splendid! But I suppose you miss him."

Bertha said grimly, "I got along all right before he came to work for me, and I guess I can get along all right now."

"You'll keep the partnership alive?"

"It'll be there when he comes back," Bertha said. "Gosh, I hope nothing happens to the little bastard!"

"Oh, he'll be all right," Doctor Rindger said. "Well, good night, Mrs. Cool."

"Good night."

Bertha Cool was grinning broadly as she climbed back into the waiting taxicab.

"Where to now?" the cab driver asked.

"The Metro Hotel," Bertha said, settling her chunky figure back in the deep cushions. "And in case you don't know, I've finally climbed aboard."

"Climbed aboard?" the cab driver asked.

"The gravy train," Bertha explained, smiling triumphantly.

"Glad to hear it," the cab driver said. "I've heard the old hack called lots of things, but this is the first time anyone called it the gravy train."

"Well, I'm riding it," Bertha said. "Took a little fumbling to get aboard, but I'm on it now."

At the Metro Hotel, Bertha Cool went directly to the house telephones and said, "You have a Christopher Milbers stopping here?"

"Yes, ma'am. Room three-nineteen."

"Ring him, please."

A moment later, Bertha Cool heard Christopher Milbers's sleep-drugged voice saying, "Hello. Yes, hello. What is it?"

Bertha Cool said crisply, "I have something important for you. I'll be up in exactly one minute."

"Who is this talking?"

"Bertha Cool," she said, and hung up.

Bertha Cool marched deliberately across the lobby, entered an elevator, and said, "Third floor."

The elevator operator looked at her questioningly as though to ask her whether she was registered in the hotel, then thought better of it. Bertha, having the manner of one who knew exactly what she intended to do, strode down the hall, located the door of 319, paused, and was in the act of knocking when Christopher Milbers opened the door. "Sorry," he said, "I'd been in bed about an hour. I'm hardly dressed for company."

He was wearing pajamas, a silk robe, and sandal slippers. His eyes were puffy from sleep, and the hair which customarily was trained so carefully around the bald spot now hung forgotten and neglected over the left ear and down to the neck, giving his head a peculiar, lopsided appearance.

Bertha said, "I'm not much at beating around the bush."

"That's a very commendable trait," Milbers said, seating Bertha in the comfortable chair and perching himself on the bed where he made himself comfortable by putting pillows up against his back. "I don't mind saying it's an *exceedingly* commendable trait."

"All right," Bertha said with machine-gun-like rapidity and precision. "Let's get down to brass tacks."

"I see no reason why we shouldn't."

"Your cousin left an estate of—how much?"

"I wouldn't know offhand, Mrs. Cool. Does it enter into the situation at all?"

"Yes."

"I would say at least half a million, perhaps more."

"You're cut off with ten thousand?"

"Exactly, Mrs. Cool, and you'll pardon me if I point out that this is not the important news which necessitated getting me up in the middle of the night. Both of us have known it for some little time."

"I understand. I'm just laying the foundation."

"Please consider the foundation as having been completely laid. I think it's quite time to go ahead with the superstructure."

Bertha said, "All right, the will's ironclad. I don't know how they did it. You don't know how they did it. Personally, I don't believe your cousin ever made any such will of his own volition. It looks very much as though he'd been cornered and forced to write the second page the way some other person, or persons, wanted it. Probably they had some blackmail strangle hold on him."

"That hardly agrees with the testimony of Miss Dell and with that of Paul Hanberry."

"It depends on the argument that was used," Bertha said. "The right sort of blackmail might have accomplished wonders. This Myrna Jackson who rooms with Josephine Dell was virtually forced upon Miss Dell by your cousin. She also knows the housekeeper. The whole thing looks fishy to me. She's apparently an attractive girl, and she's mixed up in this whole business some way. As far as Paul is concerned, I wouldn't trust him as far as I could throw an election promise by the tail."

"Yes, I'm inclined to agree with you there, but please get to the point, Mrs. Cool. You said you were going to be straightforward and not indulge in any beating around the bush."

Bertha said, "Your cousin was murdered."

Milbers's face showed his astonishment. It was a moment before he could regain his composure. "Mrs. Cool, that's a very strong statement."

"I know it's a strong statement, but your cousin was poisoned. He was given poison in his breakfast on the day he died, and he had all the symptoms of arsenic poisoning."

"It seems incredible. You're certain?"

"Practically."

"You have proof?"

"Hell, no! The point is that if we go to work, we can *get* the proof."

"Oh," Milbers said, a subtle change coming in his voice. "I thought you said you had proof."

"No. I said I was practically certain he was poisoned. So far it's all circumstantial, but I think I've got enough right now to get the D.A. to exhume your cousin's body for a checkup to see whether death actually wasn't caused by arsenic."

Milbers said, "Oh, come, Mrs. Cool. After all, that's getting the cart somewhat before the horse. I think you can appreciate that I wouldn't consider having any such step taken unless there was some definite, tangible proof that I personally considered absolutely ironclad."

Bertha said, "Well, I think I can get the proof. I've got enough at least so they'll start questioning Nettie Cranning and the Hanberrys. It'll take a little work on my part, but I think I can get the whole thing lined up and ready to dump in the D.A.'s lap in four or five days or perhaps a week."

"After all," Christopher pointed out, "this is rather an unusual situation. Exactly what did you have in mind, Mrs. Cool?"

Bertha said, "If they killed him, they can't inherit his property. Even if only one of them was in on the job and the others helped, none of them can take anything under the will. That would leave you, as the only living relative, sitting pretty. Now, I'd be willing to gamble. I'd take, say ten per cent of what you get out of the estate and do all of the detective work to make out a perfect case."

Christopher Milbers pushed the tips of his fingers together, placed the middle fingers directly beneath his chin, and frowned at Bertha Cool over the tops of his spread fingers.

"Well?" Bertha asked.

"That opens up a very, very peculiar situation, Mrs. Cool."

"Of course it does. Why did you suppose I came up here and got you out of bed?"

"Of course, if my cousin was murdered, I want justice to be done."

Bertha nodded, and then added, "And don't forget the half a million dollars that's thrown in for seeing justice done."

"I'm not forgetting it, but—well—"

"Go ahead," Bertha said. "Out with it."

"You think that it would take you some time to work up a case?"

"Naturally. I can't go out and drag something like that out of thin air."

"But you have *some* evidence?"

"Some."

"And you would want me to employ you to develop the rest?"

Bertha said, "Nix on that employment business. You and I'll make an ironclad contract by which I'll take a percentage of whatever you get from the estate."

Milbers said, "I had quite a conference with Mrs. Cranning earlier in the evening. She's really very different from what I had at first concluded."

"And her daughter?"

"A very beautiful and interesting young woman."

"I see. How about Paul Hanberry?"

Christopher Milbers's forehead puckered into a frown. "Rather antisocial," he said. "Much opposed to the existing scheme of things. Somewhat a case of maladjustment."

Bertha said, "I wouldn't have to use words like that in talking about him. Just about four words would wrap him up in a package as far as I'm concerned."

"Well, in a way my negotiations were with him, but my contacts were primarily with Mrs. Cranning."

"Okay, okay," Bertha said impatiently. "I take it that you patched up your little personal spat, and all that. But if they murdered your cousin, that's something else again."

"Quite."

"All right. That's the dish I'm offering you."

"Unfortunately, however, Mrs. Cool, it would make no difference in regard to the property."

"What?" Bertha jerked her head around so as to stare straight at him.

"That happens to be the situation. Late this evening, I reached an agreement with the other parties involved; an agreement which I consider, under the circumstances, was eminently fair. I am, of course, not obligated to tell you the specific terms of that agreement, but because of the peculiar circumstances and knowing that I can depend upon your discretion, I will divulge the general basis of agreement. Josephine Dell will take her specific legacy. In order to avoid a contest of the will and any possible litigation, with all of the resulting hard feelings, recriminations, and, above all, the delay, the parties have agreed that the residue of the estate, whatever it may be after paying the expenses of the funeral, the current bills, and the legacy to Josephine Dell, will be divided four ways equally. In other words, distribution will be made to the residuary legatees under the will; but, by this agreement, they have conveyed to me a share sufficient to make the total amount which I receive over and above my specific legacy equal to a one-fourth interest in the estate. That will give me, roughly, a hundred thousand net. It's not quite as simple as that, but the lawyers have managed to work it out and—"

"You've already signed that agreement?" Bertha asked.

"We've all signed it."

"That only relates to a contest of the will," Bertha said. "If I can prove they murdered him—"

"No, you don't understand. The agreement contains a clause that neither party will do anything which would, in any way, jeopardize the rights of any of the other parties or directly or indirectly result in depriving them of the benefit of the settlement. To hire you would be, under the circumstances, I'm afraid, a violation of the agreement—at least, of the spirit of the agreement. No, Mrs. Cool, I can hardly believe that Mrs. Cranning, or her daughter, Eva, could ever have been party to what you have suggested. It is, of course, possible that Paul Hanberry, without the knowledge of any of the others, has managed to expedite his inheritance. But as far as the others are concerned, it is absolutely out of the question. I will admit, Mrs. Cool, that people are greedy. They are impulsive. At times they are tricky, but to think for a moment that Mrs. Cranning or her daughter would poison my cousin—no, Mrs. Cool, it is absolutely, utterly unthinkable."

"Well, suppose Paul poisoned him and they found out about it afterward?"

"No, you don't understand, Mrs. Cool. In the event that the public authorities, of their own accord, started an investigation, the situation would, of course, be different; but if it should appear that any of the parties were inconvenienced in any way *by some action I had taken, or was taking* in connection with some investigation which might have, as one of its results, a different division of the estate from that mentioned in the agreement—no, Mrs. Cool, I couldn't take a chance on doing it. Frankly, I consider that I have made a *very* advantageous settlement."

"I guess so," Bertha Cool said savagely. "When a bunch of murderers can bribe a man not to investigate the murder of a relative—"

Milbers held up his hand, palm outward as though he had been a traffic officer stopping a stream of oncoming traffic. "Just *one* moment, Mrs. Cool, *pull-ease,*" he said. "I am mentioning only about hiring you. So far as any investigation made by the authorities is concerned, that, of course, would be through no volition on my part, and would in no way subject me to any criticism. But to employ you, to actually pay money directly or on a percentage basis to you as an investigator in order to dig up some evidence of that sort, that would cost me exactly one hundred thousand dollars. No, Mrs. Cool, I couldn't consider it, not for a moment. I know my lawyer would thumbs-down your proposition in a minute. He'd censure me for even discussing the matter."

"It's a slick dodge," Bertha said. "They blackmailed him into making this will; then they poisoned him. Then they make a 'compromise' with you so their scheme won't be discovered. It's a hell of a note!"

"But I can't think they resorted to blackmail any more than they did to murder. To tell you the truth, I know my cousin wrote that will. His remarks contained in it are typical. I resent them, but I *know* now that he never intended me to get a penny more than that ten thousand. This agreement is a windfall so far as I'm concerned."

"Did they come to you, or did you go to them?"

"They came to me."

"Sure. Rob a man, kill him, and soften up his heir with a hundred grand so there'll be no investigation! Pretty slick!"

"There's nothing to prevent you going to the authorities, Mrs. Cool."

Bertha said angrily, "Phooey! The authorities wouldn't get to first base with the thing—and where would there be anything in it for me on that basis?"

"Well, of course, Mrs. Cool, if you have some evidence that—"

"What I have, I have," Bertha Cool said, getting up out of the chair. "I make my living by selling my knowledge."

"If you have anything in which you think the police should be interested, it is your duty to go to them. If you have any knowledge it is your duty—"

Bertha said, "In other words, you won't put a red cent on the line. You're going to sit tight, but you'd like to see that the police get some anonymous tip that'll start them making an investigation. I suppose you're trying now to get *me* to stick my neck out and go to the police on a thank-you basis."

"It would be the proper thing to do," Milbers said. "If, as a citizen, you have any knowledge concerning a crime, or even any clues which remotely indicate—"

Bertha started for the door saying, "I'll get out and let you get dressed. There's a drugstore on the corner with a phone booth."

"I'm afraid I don't understand you," Milbers said.

"The hell you don't," Bertha announced grimly. "Within ten minutes after I'm out of here, the police will get an anonymous call telling them that Harlow Milbers was poisoned and suggesting that they look up the death certificate, talk with the doctor, and then exhume the body in order to get proof. Then you can hang up, come back here, and go to bed with that smug smile wrapped all over your face. It'll have cost you five cents for the telephone call, and that's all."

"But, my *dear* Mrs. Cool. You don't understand—"

Bertha reached the door in two quick strides, jerked it open, and slammed it shut on the rest of Milbers's speech.

The taxi which had brought Bertha to the hotel was waiting at the curb as Bertha came out.

The cab driver touched his cap. "All right, ma'am," he said with an engaging smile. "The gravy train is waiting."

"Gravy train!" Bertha said, glowering the smile right off of his face. "Gravy train, hell! Gravy train, my eye!"

Chapter Twenty

1942 AUG 31

VALLEJO, CALIFORNIA

(NIGHT LETTER COLLECT)

BERTHA COOL, CONFIDENTIAL INVESTIGATIONS
DREXEL BUILDING
LOS ANGELES, CALIFORNIA

KEY CLUE TO ENTIRE SITUATION IS FACT THAT INTERMUTUAL INDEMNITY COMPANY SEEKS TO GET RELEASE THROUGH YOU. THIS INDICATES THEY DO NOT HAVE NAME AND ADDRESS OF INJURED PARTY. ACCORDING TO WITNESS, JOSEPHINE DELL GAVE DRIVER OF CAR THAT STRUCK HER HER NAME, ADDRESS, AND PERMITTED DRIVER TO TAKE HER TO HER HOME. SITUATION SEEMS UTTERLY IMPOSSIBLE. ONE POSSIBLE EXPLANATION IS THAT DRIVER HAD BEEN DRINKING BUT WAS SUFFICIENTLY GLIB TO KEEP IT CONCEALED UNTIL AFTER DELL GOT IN AUTOMOBILE. DELL MIGHT THEN HAVE MADE DRIVER STOP CAR AND PUT HER OUT BEFORE GETTING HOME. INVESTIGATE THIS ANGLE. SUGGEST YOU RUN BLUFF ON INSURANCE COMPANY, TELLING THEM DRIVER BADLY INTOXICATED AND SEE WHAT HAPPENS. FOR SOME REASON, JOSEPHINE DELL IS NOT TELLING YOU ENTIRE TRUTH. REGARDS.

DONALD LAM

Chapter Twenty-One

BERTHA SAID indignantly to Elsie Brand, "Take a telegram to Donald— Your telegram absolutely, utterly cockeyed. Have talked with Josephine Dell who says man perfect gentleman, drove her home, solicitous over welfare. Can think of plenty of crazy things myself which don't coincide with facts without paying for collect messages containing cockeyed theories. Suggest you devote attention exclusively to winning war. Have no further connection with case. Parties have all made settlement, leaving agency out in the cold."

Bertha hesitated a moment, then said to Elsie Brand, "Read that back to me."

Elsie read it back.

"Type that up and sign my name to it," Bertha said, "and—"

She broke off as the door from the corridor opened. The tall, grave, dignified young man from the Intermutual Indemnity Company bowed gravely. "Good morning, Mrs. Cool."

"*You* again," Bertha said.

"A most unfortunate situation has developed. May I talk with you at once, Mrs. Cool?"

"Come on in," Bertha said.

"Shall I send that telegram?" Elsie asked.

"Yes, write it out, but let me read it before it goes out. Ring for a messenger."

Bertha Cool led the way into her private office. Fosdick, the insurance adjuster, settled himself comfortably in the chair, brought up his leather briefcase, rested it on his lap, and wrapped his arms around the top of it, using the briefcase as an armrest. "A *most* unfortunate situation has arisen," he repeated.

Bertha didn't say anything.

After a moment, Fosdick went on. "Did you, by any chance, know a man named Jerry Bollman?"

"What's *he* got to do with it?"

"He promised us to arrange a complete settlement—for our own figure, one thousand dollars. He made us promise that we wouldn't question what became of the money. In other words, he could turn over a less amount to the injured party if he desired. We didn't care, just so we got a complete release supported by an ample legal consideration. The injured party, once she had signed that release, could divide the money any way she wanted to, or she could permit some other person to collect the money for her if she desired.

"Mr. Bollman seemed absolutely confident of his ability to secure such a release. In fact, it seemed he had quite an interest in the injured party. He was, I believe, going with her roommate and intended to marry her soon."

"Bollman told you that?" Bertha Cool asked.

Fosdick nodded.

"Give you any names?"

"No. He just referred to the young woman as the injured party, and the other young woman as the roommate. He told a very convincing, straightforward story, however."

"And you fell for it?"

Fosdick's eyebrows rose.

Bertha Cool said, "You're young. You're just out of Harvard or some other law school that's given you a superiority complex. You think you know it all. For heaven's sake, snap out of it!"

"I *beg* your pardon."

"Skip it."

Fosdick's manner was that of a complete martyr. He managed to convey the impression that the customer was always right, that he wouldn't even try to defend himself. He said demurely, "I have no doubt Mr. Bollman could have substantiated his story. Unfortunately, however, I see from this morning's paper that Mr. Bollman was killed last night. It is, of course, regrettable from the standpoint of society and—"

"And the relatives of the dead man," Bertha Cool pointed out. "But as far as you're concerned, it's just a plain calamity. Well, I don't think Bollman would have done anything except take you for a ride, and keep stringing you along. You know damn well you can't settle a case like that for a thousand dollars."

"Why not?"

Bertha Cool laughed and said, "A man so drunk he could hardly see where he was going knocks down a pretty girl, gives her a brain concussion, and *you* want to settle for a thousand bucks."

Bertha Cool's voice dripped with sarcasm.

Fosdick said, "We are making no admissions and no concessions whatever, Mrs. Cool, but we definitely do not agree with you concerning the statement that our insured was intoxicated."

Bertha laughed sarcastically. "Your man was so dead drunk," she said, *"that he can't even remember the name and address of the woman whom he struck."*

"I don't think that's fair," Fosdick said with the slow speech of one who is meticulously choosing his words. "The young woman became hysterical and was hardly accountable for her actions."

"And your man couldn't even remember where he took her," Bertha said.

"Pardon, Mrs. Cool, but the young lady was so hysterical that she refused to permit the insured to carry her all the way home, nor would she tell him where she lived when she finally got out of the automobile."

The door of the private office opened. Elsie Brand came in with the telegram. "If you'll just check this over," she said, "the messenger boy is in the outer office."

Bertha Cool snatched at the telegram and slid it under the blotter of her desk. "Give the boy ten cents," she said. "I'm not going to send the telegram just now."

"Ten cents?" Elsie Brand asked.

"Well," Bertha conceded reluctantly. "Make it fifteen. I'm busy and don't disturb me. I'll send this telegram later."

She turned back to Fosdick as soon as the door of the office had closed. "What's the use of beating around the bush? Your man was drunk. He was too drunk to be driving the car. Not only did he knock this girl down, but when he tried to drive her home, it became very apparent he was too drunk to pilot the car, so she had to get out. Personally, I would say you were lucky if you got out of it for under twenty thousand dollars."

"Twenty thousand dollars!"

"Exactly."

"Mrs. Cool, are you crazy?"

"I'm not crazy. You are. I know what a jury will do. Apparently you don't."

Fosdick said, "Well, of course, juries at times are emotional, but unfortunately, their conduct is subject to a certain regulatory supervision by the appellate court."

"A jury might make it fifty. I don't know. You don't know."

Fosdick laughed. "Come, come, Mrs. Cool. Your client wasn't damaged very greatly."

"No?" Bertha Cool asked with a rising inflection. "You think not?"

She saw that this worried Fosdick. "We feel that under the circumstances our own physician should be given an opportunity to examine the young woman."

"All in good time," Bertha said.

"What do you mean by that?"

"You can get a court order."

"But we don't *want* to go to court."

"I mean after you get dragged into court, you can get a court order."

"Are we going to be dragged into court?"

"You don't think for a minute that we're going to let your man pull a stunt like that, and then simply send him a box of candy or a birthday card, do you?"

"Aren't you being a bit unreasonable, Mrs. Cool?"

"I don't think so."

"Look here. Suppose we settle this thing on a basis that will *really* make you some money. Your client's injuries didn't amount to much, but, for obvious reasons, we dislike very much to go to court. Suppose we say three thousand dollars cash, right on the nail?"

Bertha threw back her head and laughed.

"I'll tell you what I'll do," Fosdick said, leaning forward. "I'll make it five."

Bertha, afraid to let him see her eyes, said, "You don't realize how ridiculous you are."

"But five thousand! Surely, Mrs. Cool, that's an *enormous* settlement."

"You think so?"

"What are you expecting to get?"

Bertha looked at him then. "All the traffic will bear," she said.

"You've got the offer now," Fosdick announced, getting to his feet. "That's the extreme limit. I was going to come up to three today and not go up to five until after suit had been filed. Those were my instructions. I've taken it on myself to give you the break and let you have my final offer now."

"Nice of you," Bertha said.

"You have my card," Fosdick announced with dignity. "You can telephone me when you're ready to accept."

"Don't stick around waiting for the phone to ring."

"And," Fosdick announced, "needless to say, this is an offer of compromise. It is not permissible in evidence. It is not an admission of liability, and, unless it is accepted within a reasonable time, it will be withdrawn."

With elaborate carelessness, Bertha said, "Withdraw it now if you want to. It's okay by me."

Fosdick pretended not to hear her, but left the room with the greatest dignity.

Bertha Cool waited only until she felt certain he had reached the elevator; then she bustled out to the outer office. "Elsie, take a telegram to Donald."

"Another one?"

"Yes."

Elsie Brand held her pencil poised over the notebook.

Bertha Cool started dictating a telegram.

DONALD DEAR YOU HAVE BEEN VERY NICE AND THOUGHTFUL TO SEND BERTHA ALL OF YOUR IDEAS. MY VERY BEST THANKS. DONALD LOVER TELL ME WHY SHOULD JOSEPHINE DELL LIE TO ME ABOUT THE ACCIDENT? WHY SHOULD SHE BE WILLING TO SACRIFICE A FAT SETTLEMENT IN ORDER TO KEEP FROM TELLING EXACTLY WHAT HAPPENED AT THE TIME OF THE ACCIDENT? WIRE BERTHA COLLECT. LOTS OF LOVE AND BEST WISHES TO YOU.

"Is that," Elsie Brand asked dryly, "all?"

"That's all."

"And that other telegram. It's in on your desk I believe—do you want to send that?"

"Good heavens, no!" Bertha said. "Take that telegram, tear it up, put it in the wastebasket. Even tear that page out of your notebook. I must have been terribly angry when I dictated it. Donald certainly is a smart little devil."

Elsie Brand's smile was enigmatic. "Was there," she asked, "anything else?"

"That," Bertha announced, "is all."

Chapter Twenty-Two

1942 AUG 31

VALLEJO, CALIFORNIA

(STRAIGHT MESSAGE COLLECT)

BERTHA COOL, CONFIDENTIAL INVESTIGATIONS
   DREXEL BUILDING
      LOS ANGELES, CALIFORNIA
SUGGEST ASKING HER ROOMMATE. REGARDS.

DONALD LAM

Chapter Twenty-Three

THE MANAGER of the Bluebonnet Apartments opened the door and said, "Good afternoon. We have some very nice single apartments, one particularly choice with a—" She broke off as she recognized Bertha Cool.

Bertha said, "Just a moment, please. I might be able to make you some money."

The manager hesitated, thought that over and said, "Well?"

Bertha said, "I'm looking for someone, and if you can help me find her, I think my client would be grateful—financially."

"Who?" the woman asked.

"The young woman who moved in with Josephine Dell."

"You mean Myrna Jackson."

117

"Yes."

"What do you want her for?"

Bertha Cool opened her purse, took out a card and gave it to the manager. "She's a witness to an automobile accident. I'm running an investigating bureau."

"How much?"

"Ten dollars."

"When?"

"As soon as I find the party."

"That's taking a long gamble for a small sum."

Bertha Cool gave the manager her best smile. "You don't have to do much. Just tell me what you know about her."

"All right, come in."

The manager led the way to a ground-floor apartment, indicated a chair for Bertha, opened a drawer containing a file of cards, and selected a card which had names and figures on it.

"It was exactly a month ago," she said, "that she moved in. The maid told me that another name had been placed next to that of Josephine Dell on the directory. I asked Miss Dell about it the next night. She said that a friend of the man for whom she was working had moved in with her. I told her that the rent had been fixed on the basis of single tenancy, and she got mad and wanted to know what difference it made to me how many people were in there. She said that she'd paid the rent and that was all there was to it; that if two people lived in a single apartment, it made it inconvenient for them, but it didn't hurt the apartment any.

"As a matter of fact," the manager said, "I think she's right, but I don't make the rules of the place. I only enforce them. A bank owns it, and they tell me what to do. Well, there isn't anything in the agreement under which the apartments are rented that covers it. The only thing you can do is raise the rent five dollars at the next rent day, and you have to give thirty days' notice in writing in order to do that. We have some regular printed notices, and all we have to do is fill in the number of the

118

apartment, the amount of the rent, the date, and sign them. I had a notice all prepared, and I gave it to her, notifying her that her rent would be raised five dollars. She was good and angry, but that was all there was to it."

"Did she say she'd move out?"

"Not then."

"How long has Miss Dell been here?"

"Five months yesterday."

"You've met this Myrna Jackson?"

"Yes, twice. Once shortly after that conversation when she came to me and tried to talk me out of raising the rent. I told her that it was a house rule, there was nothing I could do about it, and that I didn't own the place."

"When was the second time you met her?"

"Last night. She came in and gave me the key; said Josephine Dell had a job working for a man who did a lot of traveling and wasn't going to be here, so they were giving up the apartment. There's a provision in the signed rules by which the tenant agrees to pay a cleaning-charge on moving out of the apartment. The cleaning-charge on this apartment was five dollars. I asked Myrna Jackson about it. She said that she was not going to pay half of it, that she wasn't going to move into a place for four weeks, and then pay two dollars and a half to have it cleaned, when the person who was already in there was obligated to pay the whole five dollars anyway. It seems the girls had had some words about it. I think they finally compromised, and Myrna Jackson paid a dollar, and Josephine paid four. I know there was some kind of a settlement they worked out. I think they were both a little upset about it; but it was Myrna Jackson who finally gave me the keys and the envelope with the cleaning-charge in it. I told Miss Jackson that if she wanted to stay on in the place alone the raise in rent wouldn't be effective. Miss Jackson really seems like a nice sort, exactly the type I like for tenants."

"Did she stay?"

The manager laughed. "She did not. She said she had nothing against me personally, but that I could tell the bank that owned the place she wouldn't stay in it if it was the last apartment on earth. It seemed she'd packed up her things and moved that afternoon. She came back to adjust matters with Miss Dell and get the cleaning-charge straightened out. Miss Jackson seemed rather angry. I gathered the two girls had had some words."

"And she left a forwarding address?" Bertha asked.

"There's ten dollars in it for me?"

"Yes."

"When I give the address?"

"No. When I find her."

"How do I know you'll tell me when you find her?"

"You don't," Bertha said.

"Well—all right. It's the Maplehurst out on Grand Avenue. Miss Jackson is really a very nice girl. She told me several times she thought the rule was unreasonable, but that she certainly didn't hold anything against me. Josephine Dell, however, was different. She was angry at me personally. She left in a huff and wouldn't even come in to see me. I got that much out of Myrna Jackson. Made her admit it. It's all right, as far as I'm concerned. Some day that Dell woman will want to get in another apartment, and when they ring up and ask me what kind of a tenant she is, I'll tell them."

"Anything wrong with her?" Bertha asked.

"That business of crabbing over rules is enough, but there are other things I could say. Not that I want to say anything against her character, but then—"

"What?" Bertha asked.

The manager sniffed. "She worked for a much older man than she? A man who walked with a slight limp and used a cane?"

"I believe so, yes."

"Humph, I thought so."

"Why? Anything wrong?"

"Oh, I wouldn't say anything was wrong, but he came to call on her two or three times, and—well, I'm not saying anything at all, but after all I've done for that girl, she certainly has no business getting sore at me because

I live up to the rules of the place. Anyhow, that isn't what we were talking about. You go to the Maplehurst Apartments, and you'll find Myrna Jackson—but don't you let on that you got her address from me, because Miss Jackson told me that there was a young man who was pestering her a lot and she didn't care about him having her address. I told her I'd keep it confidential. She just wanted mail forwarded; said I wasn't to let anyone at all have the address."

Bertha Cool said, "I'll have my client send you a check as soon as I locate her."

"Well, that's where she is, so you might just as well have your client send a check now."

"My client," Bertha said, "isn't built that way. He pays me for results and not until I get them."

"Well, I know how it is. I work for a bank myself. But you'll find her there, and you won't let on where you got the information from, will you?"

"Certainly not."

Bertha Cool, the gleam of a hunter in her eye, took a cab to the Maplehurst Apartments on Grand Avenue.

The woman who ran the apartments, an angular woman with hair the color of molasses taffy that had been slightly burned before being pulled, eyed Bertha with suspicion. "Myrna Jackson?" She had never heard of the woman. There was no one there by that name. She knew nothing whatever about it. If Bertha Cool wanted to write a letter and leave it there in case a Miss Jackson *should* take an aparment later on, Miss Jackson would get the letter. There were several vacancies in the building, but at present she knew no Myrna Jackson.

Bertha felt the woman was lying, but, for the moment, there was nothing she could do about it except pretend to be completely taken in and retire to plan an additional campaign.

The afternoon newspapers carried big headlines: *Blind Beggar Sought by Police.*

A job printer made a quick job of knocking out some stationery for Bertha Cool. By using ink which dried almost instantaneously, he was able to get her half a dozen sheets of stationery reading, BANK NIGHT SUPER DRAWING, INC., *Drexel Building, Los Angeles, California.*

Bertha took the stationery back to her office building, arranged with the elevator starter to take care of mail, and then went to her own office where she dictated a letter:

Dear Miss Jackson:

In order to keep alive an interest in bank night, an association of motion picture theaters has arranged to contribute a small percentage into a large fund on which every sixty days there is a super drawing. It is, of course, necessary to take extraordinary precautions to see that the winnings are paid to the right person. If you can, therefore, convince us that you were the person who registered at one of our member theaters during the past three months, we will give you some information which will doubtless cause you a great deal of pleasure. However, please bear in mind that since this entire matter is gratuitous and in addition to any bank night sponsored by any member theater, the entire system of awards is handled purely as a gratuitous disbursement. There is no right whatever on the part of any person whose name is drawn to receive anything.

> *Very truly yours,*
> *Bank Night Super Drawing, Inc.*
> *by*

"You can sign that, Elsie," Bertha Cool said. "I've arranged with the elevator starter to take care of any inquiries and see that they're passed along all right."

"How about using the mail to defraud?" Elsie Brand asked.

"Pish. When she shows up, we'll give her twenty-five dollars and tell her it's a gratuitous disbursement."

"Think she'll show up?"

"I'll say she will. She'll read that letter and think she's won about five thousand dollars, but someone is trying to gyp her out of it. Unless I miss my guess, Myrna Jackson has something she's keeping very much under cover. She is not going to make any squawks to the postal authorities nor anyone else, and when *I* get done with her, she's going to be a very, very good little girl."

Elsie Brand whipped the letter out of the typewriter, picked up her fountain pen, and signed it. "Under your orders," she said.

"Under my orders," Bertha Cool acknowledged reluctantly.

Chapter Twenty-Four

SERGEANT SELLERS settled himself comfortably in Bertha Cool's office and regarded her with a quiet skepticism which Bertha Cool found hard to combat.

"This blind man, Rodney Kosling," the sergeant said. "Know where he is?"

"No, of course not."

"Client of yours?"

"He was. As I told you, I did a small job for him."

"Satisfactorily?"

"I hope so."

"He might come back to you in case he wanted something else done?"

"I hope so."

"Peculiar problem when you're dealing with a blind man," Sellers went on. "You can't exactly get what you want on him."

"How do you mean?"

"Well, with an ordinary man, when it's blazoned all over the headlines of the newspapers that the police are looking for him and he still continues to stay away, you feel that you have something on him. With a blind man, it's different. He can't see the newspapers. You know there's *just* a chance Rodney Kosling may not know anything at all about what has happened and may not know that the police are looking for him."

"That's probably it," Bertha said, just a little too eagerly, as she realized as soon as the words were out of her mouth.

Sergeant Sellers went on without letting her comment divert him in the least, "I say there's a chance of it—about one chance in twenty."

"You mean about one chance in twenty that he knows you want him?"

"No, I mean about one chance in twenty he *doesn't* know we want him."

"I don't get you," Bertha said.

"Well, let's look at it this way. We've eliminated nearly all of these beggar peddlers. Time was when you used to see a lot of them on the street—people going around with tin cups and guitars. It got to be a racket. We kicked them all out except half a dozen who had done things for the police in times past or had some political pull. These people have very definite locations where they're permitted to work. When they die off, there won't be any others to take their places. We're getting the city cleaned up. At least, we're trying to."

"Well?" Bertha asked.

"How do you suppose those blind people get to work?"

"I don't know," Bertha Cool said. "I'd never thought of it."

"They have a nifty little club," Sergeant Sellers said. "It's a co-operative affair. They jointly own an automobile and hire a chauffeur. He drives around, picks them up in the morning according to a regular routine, takes them out and spots them, and calls for them at a fixed hour at night. They ride out to the chauffeur's house. His wife has a nice hot dinner fixed for them. They eat and chat, and then the chauffeur drives them home one at a time."

"Well," Bertha said, thinking it over, "I can understand that. If I'd stopped to think, I'd have known there must have been something like that; that it was handled somewhat along those lines. He can't drive a car, and he can't very well take streetcars to and from his place of business. Hiring a private car and chauffeur and a housekeeper would be pretty much of an impossibility. Who keeps his house, anyway?"

"The chauffeur's wife. She goes around to the houses in rotation and cleans 'em up once a week. The rest of the time the chaps get along by themselves. And you'd be surprised at how much they're able to do regardless of being blind."

"Who's the chauffeur?" Bertha asked.

"Man by the name of Thinwell, John A. Thinwell. He and his wife have pretty good references; seem to be pretty well thought of. Tell a straightforward story."

"What is it?"

"These chaps don't work Sundays. On Sundays, they all get together around three o'clock at Thinwell's house, listen to music on the radio, sit and talk, and get acquainted. Thinwell serves 'em a dinner around seven and then takes 'em home.

"Sunday about noon, Thinwell got a telephone call from Kosling. He seemed rather excited or disturbed and was talking rapidly. He said he wasn't going to be home all day, couldn't attend their little club meeting, and that Thinwell was not to call for him.

"Thinwell had to go right by the house anyway to pick up another one of the members, so he stopped in. That was about ten to three. The place was deserted, all right, and Kosling had left the door propped open a few inches so his tame bat could get in and out."

"Did Thinwell look inside?" Bertha asked.

"He says he just peeped inside the door. There's something strange about that, too. He said Kosling's pet bat was flying around inside the room. That's unusual. Unless bats are disturbed, they fly around at night. Now *why* should this bat have been flying around at three in the afternoon?"

"He must have been disturbed," Bertha said.

"Exactly," Sellers agreed. "And what disturbed him?"

"I'll bite. What did?"

"It must have been the person who was putting up the trap gun. That brings up another interesting thing."

"What?"

"I think the trap gun was set up by a blind man."

"What makes you think so?"

"Because of the way it was set up. In the first place there was no attempt at concealment. The thing stuck out as big as an elephant, right where it could be seen by anyone entering the room. In the second place, in pointing the gun, the man who set it up didn't squint along the sights the way a man with vision would have done. He tied a thread along the barrel, pulled that thread tight, and used it to tell him where the charge was going. That's one way of sighting a gun. It's the hard way.

"Ordinarily when a man is murdered, we make a study of his contacts, of the people with whom he associates. Nine times out of ten, when robbery isn't the motive, the murderer is someone who has had intimate contact with him. Nine-tenths of Kosling's associates are blind.

"Now then, those associates gathered at around three forty-five at Thinwell's house, had their usual dinner and social gathering, and went home around nine. Therefore, if one of these blind men did it, he must have set the trap gun *before* the party, which accounts for the bat flying around the room."

"Curtains down?" Bertha asked.

"Yes. That seems to be a peculiar obsession of blind men. They have a tendency to keep their curtains down."

"Why?"

"Search me. Thinwell says he's noticed it with Kosling in particular, several times."

"You say Kosling telephoned Thinwell?"

"Yes."

"Call from a pay station?" Bertha asked.

"Yes."

"How would he dial a number?"

"That's easy. You don't realize how sensitive those people are with their fingers. They could manipulate a dial phone just about as quickly as you could, once they knew the number. Otherwise, all they'd have to do is dial Operator, explain the situation, and have operator get them the number."

Sergeant Sellers's eyes caught Bertha's and held them in a cold, steely grip. "There are two theories to work on. One of them is that Jerry Bollman wanted to call on this blind man, or else wanted to get something out of the place. He went out, found the door open on account of this pet bat, and started exploring."

"What's the other theory?" Bertha asked noncommittally.

"The other theory is that Kosling went out with Bollman; that Bollman took him to dinner. When Bollman had finished with him, he took him home, led the way up the walk, holding the blind man's arm, probably lighting his own way with a flashlight. Bollman flung open the door, stepped inside, and—BANG!"

Bertha gave a quick, nervous start.

"Just acting things out for you," Sergeant Sellers said, and smiled.

"Sounds like very fair reasoning," Bertha said, "taking everything into consideration."

"The last theory," Sergeant Sellers said, "sounds a lot better to me—provided there was something Bollman wanted from this blind man, some information or something. Any idea what it could have been?"

Bertha hesitated over that.

"Something that might have been connected in some way with the thing Kosling employed you about in the first place," Sergeant Sellers prompted, and, as Bertha failed to take the bait, he added significantly, "something that perhaps had to do with a woman."

"What sort of a woman?" Bertha asked quickly.

"There," Sellers admitted, "you have me stumped. It wouldn't be a woman who would be interested from an amorous angle unless she was a gold digger pure and simple."

"Make it simple," Bertha said. "The other's superfluous."

Sellers grinned.

"Well," Bertha said, "then what?"

"Then," Sellers retorted, "we come down to the plain

business theory. Kosling might have had some information Bollman wanted to get."

Elsie Brand put her head in the door. "Could you get on the telephone, Mrs. Cool?"

Bertha Cool looked at her, caught a peculiar significance in Elsie's glance, said, "Just a moment," to Sellers, and picked up the telephone.

Central's voice said, "San Bernardino is calling and wants you to pay for the message."

"Well, they've got a crust," Bertha Cool said. "The answer to that is very simple, very short, and very sweet. I don't accept collect calls."

She had just started to hang up the receiver when Elsie Brand, who was also on the line, said, "I understand it's a Mr. Kosling calling, Mrs. Cool."

Bertha had the telephone receiver almost an inch from her ear. She wondered if Sergeant Sellers had heard. He gave no sign of having done so.

Bertha said, "Well, under the circumstances, it's okay. Put your party on."

She heard a click, and almost immediately the peculiar, unmistakable voice of the blind man saying, "Hello, is this Mrs. Cool?"

"Yes."

"Don't let anyone know where I am. Don't mention any names over the telephone, understand?"

"Yes."

"I understand the police are looking for me."

"Yes."

"Bad?"

"I think so."

"Could you come out and get me without letting anyone know anything about it?"

"That would be rather difficult."

"It's very important."

"Give me the address."

"The Sequoia Hotel in San Bernardino."

"What name?"

"I don't know. You see, I can't read. I didn't have a

chance to see the register. I *may* be registered under my own name."

"That," Bertha said, "is bad."

"I can give you the room number."

"What?"

"Four-twenty."

"That's all I need. Wait there until you hear from me."

"I'd like to see you just as soon as I can."

"All right, just wait there." Bertha hung up.

"You sound like a busy woman," Sergeant Sellers announced.

"Busy, hell!" Bertha said with disgust. "When people start calling you collect, that's the kind of business that enables the red-ink manufacturers to declare dividends."

"It is for a fact," Sellers agreed, smiling. "Well, here's the point, Mrs. Cool. We have reason to believe Jerry Bollman may have been with Rodney Kosling last night. Now, can you help us on that?"

"I can't do a thing. My hands are tied."

"You mean you don't have the information, or do you mean that you can't ethically betray the confidences of a client?"

Bertha hesitated for a moment and said, "I think I've answered your questions truthfully, according to the best information I have at the time, and I think they've covered this thing thoroughly."

The sergeant nodded but made no move toward leaving. He simply sat there, looking at her.

"Was Bollman driving a car?" Bertha Cool asked abruptly.

"Yes. He'd parked it two blocks away. We didn't find it until morning. It's registered in his name."

"Suppose Bollman drove Kosling home. Suppose your theory is correct, and because Bollman was dealing with a blind man, he took his arm, led him up the walk, opened the door, stepped inside, and pulled the thread which fired the gun? What happened to Kosling? How could he get anywhere?"

"There are some men in the department who think perhaps you took him somewhere, Mrs. Cool."

"Think that *I* did!" Bertha exclaimed incredulously.

"That's right."

"Well, they're cockeyed. Tell them I said so."

"You do say so?"

"Emphatically, yes."

"You didn't drive him away?"

"No."

"That trip you made by taxicab to the Kosling bungalow wasn't your *second* trip?"

"Certainly not."

"Kosling is a client of yours. He'd have called you if there'd been trouble. You wouldn't be trying to protect him, would you?"

"Aren't you funny?"

"Am I?"

"No, but you're trying to be."

"Now, when you went out to Kosling's house, you didn't by any chance have an appointment to meet Kosling and Bollman out there, did you? You didn't find Kosling gibbering with fright, telling you Bollman had been killed, and you didn't tell Kosling to go out through the back and wait for you at some appointed place, did you?"

"Heavens, no!"

Sellers put his big palms on the arms of the chair, pushed himself to his feet, looked down at Mrs. Cool, and said, "It wouldn't be nice if you were to try slipping something over. I don't know yet just what's at stake. I'll find out later. When I find out, I'll know a lot more than I do now. You understand how annoyed I'd be if it turned out you were standing between me and the solution of the murder case."

"Naturally," Bertha said.

"I guess that covers it," Sergeant Sellers announced.

"Very thoroughly," Bertha told him, and saw him as far as the door.

Bertha waited at the door of the entrance office until

she heard the clang of the elevator door; then she dashed back and said to Elsie Brand, "Get me the garage where I keep my car, Elsie. Quick!"

Elsie Brand's nimble fingers flew around the dial of the telephone. "Here you are, Mrs. Cool."

Bertha Cool took the telephone. "This is Mrs. Cool," she said. "I'm confronted with an emergency. Do you have a boy on duty who can deliver my car?"

"Why, yes, Mrs. Cool. It's only a block from your office, you know."

"I know," Bertha said impatiently, "but I don't want to pick up the car at my office."

"I see."

Bertha said, "I'm going to walk down to Seventh Street and take a streetcar west on Seventh. I'm leaving the office immediately. I want you to have a boy pick up my car and drive slowly along West Seventh. I'll get off the streetcar somewhere between Grand Avenue and Figueroa Street. I'll be waiting in a safety zone, and I'll be watching for the car. As soon as I see it come along, I'll jump into the back seat. The boy can drive me for two or three blocks until we get out of traffic, and then I'll let him out of the car and he can take a streetcar back. Do you understand?"

"Yes, Mrs. Cool."

"That," Bertha announced, "is the kind of service I like. I'm leaving at once."

"The car will leave here in just about three minutes."

"Take five," Bertha said. "I want to be certain we don't miss connections."

Bertha hung up, grabbed her hat, pushed it down on her head, and said to Elsie Brand, "Close up the office at five o'clock. If anyone asks where I am, you don't know. I went out to see a witness." She didn't even wait to make sure of Elsie Brand's nod of understanding, but hurried to the elevator, emerged into the glare of the sun-swept street, walked briskly over to Seventh Street, caught a streetcar as far as Grand Avenue, then got out and stood in the safety zone, waiting, watching traffic.

131

Apparently no one gave her more than a casual glance, nor did she notice any suspicious-looking automobiles discharge passengers, pull in to the curb, or do anything to arouse her suspicions.

She had been waiting less than two minutes when she saw a garage attendant driving her automobile, slipping along in the stream of traffic.

She signaled him, and, as he stopped, whipped the rear door open, scrambled inside, and said, "Step on it."

The lurch of the starting car threw her back against the seat cushions.

"Turn to the right on Figueroa," Bertha said. "Make a left turn on Wilshire, run four or five blocks, turn to the left, and stop in the middle of the block."

While the boy from the garage was doing this, Bertha opened her purse and started powdering her nose. She held the little mirror concealed in her hand in such a way that she could look through the rear window of the car and see the traffic behind her.

When the boy had made the left-hand turn off Wilshire, Bertha got out of the car, said, "All right, I'll take it now. You can go over to Seventh Street and get a car back. Here's carfare."

She handed him a dime; then at the expression on his face, impulsively added twenty-five cents to it.

"Thank you, Mrs. Cool."

Bertha's answer was an inarticulate grunt. She settled herself behind the steering-wheel, pulled up her skirts so that her knees were free, adjusted the rearview mirror, and waited for a good five minutes. Then she swung the car in a U-turn in the middle of the block and went back to Wilshire. She turned right to Figueroa, made a left turn, made a figure eight around two blocks, then drove to the Union Station. She parked the car, walked into the station, looked around, came back, got in her car, and drove down Macy Street.

By the time she lined out for San Bernardino, Bertha Cool was morally certain that no one was following her.

She reached Pomona just before the stores closed and

stopped long enough to purchase a cheap but substantial suitcase, a dress which would fit a tall, thin woman, a broad-brimmed hat, and a light-tan, loose-fitting coat. She fitted her purchases into the suitcase, paid for them, and carried the suitcase out to the automobile.

In San Bernardino she once more made certain that no one was following her before she parked the car in front of the hotel. She honked the horn to get the attention of a bellboy, handed him the suitcase, registered as B. Cool of Los Angeles, asked for a cheap inside room, objected to 214 as not being exactly what she wanted, and finally compromised on 381. She explained to the clerk that she might have to check out by telephone, asking the hotel to store her suitcase until she would have an opportunity to pick it up, and stated that she preferred to pay for the room in advance. Having paid a day's rent and secured a receipt signed by the clerk, she let the bellboy take her to her room.

The bellboy made a great show of opening the window, turning on the lights, raising shades, making certain there were towels on the racks.

Bertha stood by the bed watching his activities, and when he had finished, dropped a ten-cent piece into his palm, then after a moment's hesitancy, added a nickel.

"Was there anything else?" he asked.

"Nothing," Bertha said. "I'm going to take a bath and then sleep for a while. Please leave word that I'm not to be disturbed on the telephone."

Bertha hung a *Please Do Not Disturb* sign on the knob of the door, turned off the lights, locked the door, and, carrying her suitcase, found the stairway, climbed to the fourth floor, and located room 420. There was a *Please Do Not Disturb* on that doorknob.

She tapped gently on the door.

"Who is it?" Kosling's voice asked.

"Mrs. Cool."

She heard the tapping of his cane, then the sound of the bolt shooting back, and Kosling, looking old, bent, and worn, opened the door.

"Come in."

Bertha entered the room which was close with the smell of human occupancy. Kosling closed the door after her and locked it.

Bertha said, "Good heavens, it's stuffy in here. You've got the windows down, the shades drawn, and—"

"I know, but I was afraid someone would see in."

Bertha Cool went over to the window, pulled the shade to one side, then jerked the shade up, raised the windows, and said, "No one can see in. You have an outside room."

"I'm sorry," Kosling said in a patient voice. "That's one of the disadvantages of being blind. You can never tell whether you have an inside room, and there's another room right across the court from you."

"Yes," Bertha said, "I can understand that. How did you know what had happened?"

"The radio," he said, indicating a section of the room with a vague wave of his hand. "I stumbled on the radio, rather a luxury for me. They apparently have some meter arrangement by which they can charge you for the amount of time it's played."

"Yes," Bertha said. "Fifteen cents an hour."

"I turned it on and was listening to music and news broadcasts. Then I heard about it in a news broadcast."

"And what did you do?"

"Called you."

"And you'd been waiting here all that time—before you called me?"

"Yes."

"Why?"

"Bollman told me to."

Bertha said, "All right, let's talk. Tell me everything that happened."

"There isn't anything to tell you," he said. "You've got to tell me."

"Tell me all you know."

"Well, I have a chauffeur. I don't have him all by myself. There are several others who—"

"Yes, I know all about that," Bertha Cool said. "Begin from when you met Bollman."

"The first time I met him, I didn't know who he was. He dropped five silver dollars into my cup, one right after another, and—"

"Skip that," Bertha Cool said. "I know about that."

"I naturally remembered him. I remembered the sound of his step, and there's a peculiar odor about him, a rather distinctive type of tobacco. It has a certain pungent aroma."

"All right, you remembered him. When was the next time you saw him again?"

"Yesterday."

"When?"

"About noon."

"What happened?"

"He came to my house just around twelve and said, 'You don't know who I am, but I want to ask you a few questions. Answering them correctly may mean a good deal to you.' He thought I didn't know him, thought I didn't realize he was the same man who had put the five silver dollars into my cup. I never let on. When they don't want me to know, I pretend I don't know. So I just smiled and said, 'Very well, what is it?'

"Then he asked me all about you; asked me if I'd hired you and what you'd found out for me. Naturally, I didn't want to tell him too much. I was a little vague in my replies. Being a perfect stranger except for that one time when he'd dropped the money, I didn't feel like telling him all of my private affairs. I told him that he could get in touch with you, and you could tell him all about it."

"Then what?"

"Then he said that the young woman who had sent me a present wanted to see me. Unfortunately, she couldn't come to me, but if I could come to her, she'd appreciate it very much. He said that we could have dinner together and then he could drive me home after I'd seen her."

"Go ahead."

"Perhaps you don't realize how humdrum and routine our lives become. It's a peculiar type of loneliness. We're in the middle of a big city. People stream past us. We get so we know them. We hear their steps, recognize them almost as definitely as though we could see them; but they never speak to us. When they do, it's just a patronizing little expression of sympathy. You'd prefer they didn't say anything."

Bertha nodded; then realizing that he couldn't see the nod, said, "I understand. That is, I can understand enough to see what you're getting at. Go ahead. Give me the facts just as fast as you can."

"Well, naturally, I jumped at the chance to break away from my routine and enjoy some normal human companionship."

Bertha Cool, thinking that statement over, said abruptly, "You had a lot of dough on you when you came to my office. Is begging that profitable?"

He smiled. "As it happens, there is perhaps a bare existence in begging. I don't keep any books on it. My income is quite independent of that."

"Then why do you drag yourself down to sit on the sidewalk and—"

"Purely for the companionship, to feel that I'm a part of things. I got started at it when there was no other alternative. I haven't any particular education. I couldn't make friends with the class of people I wanted."

"Where did these investments of yours come from?"

"That's rather a long story."

"Make it short and give it to me."

"A man used to be rather generous with me. He said I brought him luck. He gave me a few shares in a Texas oil development—just dropped the certificate into the cup. I couldn't read it. I took his word for what it was and put it away.

"To tell you the truth, I entirely forgot about them. Then a man came to see me one day; said he'd been looking for me and that I hadn't answered his letters. Well, anyway, it seems they'd struck oil, lots of it. He

136

made me an offer for my stock. I didn't sell out. I preferred to hold it. It's paid me a steady income. Being blind, I can't write checks and have a bank account—not conveniently. I keep my money on me. I like to feel it there. When you aren't normal physically, it gives you a feeling of greater assurance to have a lot of money actually on you. A big roll of bills builds morale."

"I see. Let's get back to Bollman."

"Well, we went to an early dinner. We talked a little. He said that the girl I wanted to see was out of town. He had an appointment to take me to her and that it would be about an hour-and-a-half or a two-hour drive. I didn't think anything of it. I had confidence in him, and settled back in the car and talked with him."

"What did you talk about?"

"Oh, a variety of things—philosophy, politics—everything."

"About that automobile accident?"

"Oh, it was mentioned."

"About the work I'd done for you?"

"In a general way. He'd won my confidence by that time."

"About the presents you'd received from Josephine Dell?"

"Yes. I mentioned those."

"Then what?"

"We came here. I didn't even know what city it was. He said he'd have to do some telephoning and for me to wait in the car. I waited in the car. He came back and seemed very much disappointed, said that it was going to be quite late tonight or early tomorrow before we could see her. Something had developed. She regretted it very much and wanted him to tell me how sorry she was. We had a bite to eat. Then Bollman got me this room, said he had some work to do, and he'd see me in the morning.

"I have a watch by which I can tell time. I unscrew the crystal and feel the position of the hands. It's my only way of telling when it's daytime—to know the time. If I ever lose track of the hour, I get all mixed up—can't tell whether it's eleven in the morning or eleven at night. I slept until about nine o'clock; then I got up, dressed, and waited. It took me a while to get a bath and get dressed. This is a strange room, and I had to feel my way around until I finally got everything all listed and memorized. One thing bothered me; I couldn't tell whether the lights were on or off. I couldn't remember whether Bollman had switched them off when he went out. A man hates to make a spectacle of himself, and I didn't know but what there might be some room right across the narrow court from me, so I kept the curtains pulled down. Well, after a while, when I thought surely it was time, I picked up the telephone and asked them if they'd ring Mr. Bollman's room. They told me there was no Bollman registered. That bothered me. I don't eat very much as a rule, and I'd had a hearty dinner the day before and a bite after we got here, so I didn't eat any breakfast. I found the radio, turned it on, listened to music for a while, dozed off, woke up, and finally began to worry. Then, when I was playing the radio, a news program came on, and I heard about Bollman. Well, I didn't know *what* to do."

"You telephoned me?"

"Not until a couple of hours had elapsed. I didn't know just what to do. I was completely at a loss."

"You haven't been out of the room?"

"No, and, what's more, I haven't even dared to have them bring me anything to eat. I put a 'don't disturb' sign on the door and sat tight. If, as the radio says, the police are looking for me—well—"

"Now, we're getting to it," Bertha said. "Why don't you want the police to find you?"

"I don't mind," Kosling said, "*after* I've found out exactly what happened; but from what I heard over the radio, that trap was set for me. Bollman simply happened to walk into it. That's what I must clear up. I want to find out about who could want to kill me."

"We're coming to that," Bertha said. "It's a blind man."

138

"How do you know?"

"From the way the trap was rigged up. Sergeant Sellers has given me everything the police have on it. It's almost certain that it was a blind man who did it."

"I can't believe it's possible. I can't believe that one of my associates would do a thing like that."

"How about someone else?"

"No. My associates knew my house, the people who are in my little club. They're not *all* blind. One of them has both legs and an arm off. There's seven of us who are blind."

"That leaves six others besides yourself. Are they familiar with your house?"

"Yes. They've all been there. They've all seen Freddie."

"Who's Freddie?"

"My pet bat."

"I see. Had him long?"

"Quite a while. I leave my door open because of him."

"Well, Sellers thinks the trap was baited for you by another blind man. That leaves six suspects. Is that right?"

"I suppose so."

"Why did Bollman go to your house?"

"I can't understand. He must have left for the house just as soon as he went out of my room here in the hotel—"

"Exactly," Bertha said. "That means he'd planned to do it quite a bit earlier."

"How much earlier?"

"I don't know. Sometime on the trip out here. Sometime after leaving Los Angeles."

"Why?"

"There's only one reason. It was something you said to him, something that made it important for him to get into your house. There are only two things I can think of."

"What?"

"The flowers and the music box."

139

"Oh, I hope nothing's happened to my music box."

"I think it's all right. Did you tell Bollman about your pet bat?"

"I can't remember."

"This bat lives there in the house all the time?"

"Yes. He's very affectionate. When I come in, he always flutters up against my face and snuggles there for a while. I want pets. I like them. I can't keep a dog or cat."

"Why not?"

"Because they can't be self-supporting, and I can't wait on them. While I'm away, I'd have to leave them locked up in the house, and then the problem of feeding them, of giving a dog exercise, of letting a cat in and out—no, I have to have a pet that's self-supporting. There was an old woodshed out in the back of the house, and this bat lived in there. I finally got him tame, and now he stays in the house. I leave the door open, and he can fly in and out. It makes no difference whether I'm there or not. He can come and go and live his own life—support himself."

Bertha switched the subject abruptly. "You told Bollman that I'd located Josephine Dell for you?"

"Yes."

"Tell him you had her address?"

"I think so."

"And you're certain you told him about getting the bouquet and the music box?"

"Yes."

"That seem to excite him?"

"I don't know. I couldn't tell. His voice didn't show it. I couldn't see his expressions, you know."

"But *something* excited him. It must have. He went back to your house to get something or do something, and walked into the trap that had been set for you."

"That's the thing I can't understand."

Bertha looked up and said, "It's the most exasperating damn situation."

"What is?"

"This whole business. You've got some information that I want."

140

"What is it?"

"I don't know," Bertha said, "and the hell of it is, you don't, either. It's something that doesn't occur to you as being at all important, something that you must have mentioned in driving out here with Bollman."

"But what could it possibly be?"

"It had something to do with that automobile accident," Bertha Cool said.

"I think I've told you everything."

"That's it. You *think* you've told me everything you told Bollman. You haven't. There's something that's terribly significant, something that means a lot of money to a lot of people."

"Well, what are we going to do? Get in touch with the police and tell them the story?"

Bertha said grimly, "And have the police spill the whole thing to the papers? Not by a hell of a sight!"

"Why not?"

"Because I'm on the trail of something that's going to give me a fifty-per-cent cut of at least five thousand dollars, and if you think I'm going to toss twenty-five hundred bucks out of the window, you're crazy."

"But I don't see where that has any connection with me."

"I know you don't. That's the hard part of it. You're going to have to sit down with me and talk. Just keep on talking. Try and talk over the things you discussed with Bollman, but, no matter what it is, *keep talking.*"

"But I've got to eat. I can't get out of here, and I can't—"

"Yes, you can," Bertha said. "Come on down to my room. I've got some women's clothes that will fit you. You're going out with me as my mother. You've just had a slight stroke, and you're walking very slowly, leaning on my arm. You aren't using a cane."

"Think we can do it all right?"

"We can try."

"I would like to have it appear that—well, you know, the time I was here."

"Why?"

"So that in case—well, in case the police should accuse me of killing Bollman, I could show them that I'd been right here in the hotel all the time."

Bertha Cool pursed her lips, gave a low whistle, and then said, "Fry me for an oyster!"

"What's the matter?" Kosling asked.

Bertha said, "You haven't an alibi that's worth a damn."

"Why not? *I* couldn't drive out to Los Angeles, kill Bollman, and then drive all the way back here by myself."

"No, but you could have done all that, then had someone else drive you out here, and cook up this nice-sounding story."

"If Bollman didn't bring me out here, who did?" Kosling demanded.

Bertha Cool frowned at him. "That," she said, "is what I've been trying to think of for the last minute. But I know who Sergeant Sellers will say did it—now."

"Who?" Kosling asked.

"Me! And I've put my fist on the hotel register downstairs."

Chapter Twenty-Five

BERTHA COOL stood Kosling up on the chair and said, "Now keep your balance. Here, put up your hand. No, the other hand. Now you can reach the chandelier—now, stay perfectly still because I'm going to let go of you."

Bertha gently withdrew her hands.

"It's all right," the blind man said. "I'm all right now."

Bertha, surveying the effect, said, "But I can't have you holding your arm up that way. Wait a minute. I'll give you something else to hang onto."

She moved a high-backed chair over beside him and said, "Here, put your hand on this. Let me guide it. There it is. Now, just hold still and let me get this hem."

She pulled pins from a folded paper, thrust the heads

into her mouth, and went around the skirt, taking up the hem. When she had gone completely around the base of the garment, she stood back to survey the results and said, "I think that'll be all right. Now, let's get down."

She helped him to the floor, slipped the dress off over his head, and, sitting on the edge of the bed, did a hasty job of basting the hem into place.

"Don't you think that it might be advisable for me to get in touch with the police?" Kosling asked. "I didn't know what to do when I first heard that announcement over the radio, but the more I think of it, the more I feel—"

Bertha said with exasperation in her voice, "Now, listen, let's get this straight. Let's get it straight at once and for all. You've got some information that's worth exactly five thousand dollars. Out of that five thousand dollars I'm going to get two thousand five hundred. Something you said to Bollman gave him the tip. He went out to your house and walked into a trap someone had set for you. The police are interested in who set that trap and why. I'm interested in finding out what Bollman was after. Once the police get hold of you, they'll sew you up in a sack. To me, twenty-five hundred smacks is twenty-five hundred smacks. Now, do you understand?"

"But I can't imagine what that information was."

"The hell of it is that I can't, either," Bertha admitted, "but right now you're a walking gold mine as far as I'm concerned, so I'm going to stick closer than a brother until we get everything all cleaned up. Do you understand?"

"Yes, I understand that."

"All right, that's all you need to know. Now, come on We're going to get out of here while the getting is good You're my mother. You've had a slight stroke. We're going out for a walk. You aren't going to say anything to anyone, and in case anyone does any talking, your contribution to the conversation will be a sweet smile. All right now, here we go."

Bertha gave a few last touches to the ensemble, took

Kosling's arm, and said, "Now, I want you to lean on me. Don't act as though I was giving you guidance. Let it look as though I was giving you support. A blind person gets guidance. A person who is weak on his legs gets support. Do you understand what I mean?"

"I think so. Like this?"

"No," Bertha said, "you're just bearing down. Lean over a little bit to one side. That's it. All right now, here we go."

Bertha guided Kosling through the door, locked it, and said, "Because my room's on the third floor, we've got to make the stairs. Think you can do it all right?"

"Why, of course."

"The thing you've got to watch," Bertha said, "is that skirt. I've got the hem fixed so it's just about dragging the ground. I don't want people to see your shoes and the bottom of your pants."

"I thought you rolled my pants up."

"I did, but I left the skirt plenty long. Come on now, watch the stairs."

They negotiated the stairs safely. Bertha walked down the corridor to the elevator, rang the bell, and when the hotel's single elevator eventually came rattling up, said, "Now be careful, Mother. Watch your step getting in the elevator."

They got in without mishap except that Kosling, forgetting the wide brim on the woman's hat he was wearing, all but crushed it against the back of the elevator.

"Take it easy going down," Bertha Cool said to the elevator operator.

He laughed. "Ma'am, this cage has got only one speed —and that's easy."

They reached the lobby. The clerk looked solicitously at Bertha's "mother." The elevator operator who doubled as bellboy held the outer door open for Bertha, and Bertha Cool, standing so that her own skirt shielded any glimpse of Kosling's leg from the bellboy, helped Kosling into the automobile and closed the door. She gave the bellboy the benefit of a smile, walked around to the car, climbed in, and drove away.

"Where to?" Kosling asked.

"Riverside," Bertha said. "We go to a hotel there, and get connecting rooms."

It was beginning to get dark. Bertha switched on the headlights and drove slowly. Reaching Riverside, she went into one of the older hotels, registered as Mrs. L. M. Cushing and daughter, secured two rooms with a connecting bath, and made some ceremony of getting Kosling up to the rooms and safely ensconced.

"Now," Bertha announced, "*you're* going to stay right here, and *we're* going to talk."

At the end of an hour when Kosling felt he was completely talked out, Bertha ordered some dinner sent up from a near-by restaurant. An hour later, she went to a public telephone, called the hotel in San Bernardino, and said, "This is Mrs. Cool. The thing that I was afraid was going to happen has happened. My mother's had another stroke. I won't be able to get back to pick up my things. Please store my suitcase. You'll find that my bill is paid, and there are no telephone calls or other extras."

The clerk assured her that he regretted the nature of the occasion which prevented Bertha Cool from returning, that he trusted her mother would make a complete and prompt recovery, and assured Bertha she had nothing whatever to worry about in connection with her belongings.

Bertha thanked him, returned to the hotel, and for two more hours pumped the blind man, trying to get some bit of information out of him, going over the events of the last week with monotonous repetition, a probing search for detail.

Kosling at length became tired and irritated. "I've given you everything I have to give; told you all that I know," he said petulantly. "I'm going to sleep. I wish I'd never seen you and never interested myself in that girl at all. As a matter of fact, she—" His voice faltered as he choked off what he was going to say.

"What's that?" Bertha asked, pouncing on his unfinished sentence.

"Nothing."

"What were you going to say?"

"Oh, nothing, except that—I've been disappointed in that girl."

"What girl?"

"Josephine Dell."

"Why?"

"Well, for one thing, she never stopped by to see me. If she was able to return to work, she could certainly have stopped by long enough to say hello."

"She was working at a different place," Bertha explained. "When Harlow Milbers was alive, she was working down at that loft building where they had an office, but after his death, she had no occasion to go there. What work she did do was at his residence."

"But I still don't understand why she didn't come to see me."

"She sent you a very nice present, didn't she? Two of them, in fact."

"Yes. That music box meant a lot to me. She must have known how much I wanted to thank her personally for that."

"Can't you write her?"

"My writing isn't very good. I don't use a typewriter, and I have to grope around with a pencil. I dislike writing intensely."

"Well, why not call her up?" Bertha asked.

"That's just the point. I did. She wouldn't waste her time with me."

"Wait a minute," Bertha said. "This is something new. You say she wouldn't waste her time with you?"

"I called her up, but she wasn't in. I talked with some woman and I told her who I was. She said Miss Dell was busy right at the moment, but she would give her any message. I told her I wanted to thank Miss Dell for her gifts and that I'd wait at that number until Miss Dell called."

"Well?" Bertha asked.

"I waited and waited—for over an hour. She never called."

"Where," Bertha asked, "did you call her—at her apartment?"

"No, at the place she was working—the residence of the man she worked for. You know, Milbers."

"Just how well did you know her?" Bertha asked.

"Oh, quite well—in a way—just by talking with her, though."

"Just when she'd stop on the street?"

"That's right."

"Not much chance to establish an intimate friendship," Bertha said musingly.

"Oh, we really talked quite a bit, but just a few words at a time. She was one of the brightest spots in my day, and she knew it. Well, when she didn't call me, I called again and asked for Miss Dell, and the person who answered the phone wanted to know if I was a friend of hers and said she was busy. I remember I tried to be funny. I said I was a man who had never seen her in his life and never expected to. Well, they called her to the telephone, and I said, 'Hello, Miss Dell, this is your blind friend. I wanted to thank you for the music box.' She said, 'What music box?' and I told her the music box she had sent to her friend, the blind beggar. She told me then that she had sent me flowers and was too busy to talk, and hung up. I've been wondering if that accident hadn't affected her memory so she couldn't remember things, but for some reason she didn't want people to know about it because there was something she *had* to say she remembered. Maybe she was a witness to some contract, or perhaps she may have known—"

"Wait a minute," Bertha interrupted. "Are you certain *she* sent you the music box?"

"Oh, yes. She's the only one I had ever talked with and told about how much I liked them. I thought perhaps she was injured more seriously than she realized, so I determined to go to her—"

"How did she sound on the telephone? Her usual self?"

147

"No. Her voice was strained and harsh. She's really not right mentally. Her memory—"

"Did you tell all this to Bollman?"

"What?"

"About the telephone call and the music box and Josephine losing her memory?"

"Let me see. Yes—I guess I did."

Bertha was excited now.

"You got the music box right after she'd been hurt, is that right?"

"Yes—within a day or two."

"And how did it come?"

"A messenger brought it to me."

"And where did the messenger say he was from?"

"From the store that sold it, some antique dealer. I've forgotten the name. He said he'd received instructions to deliver it to me. He said he'd been holding it for a young lady who had paid a deposit on it and who had just recently completed—"

"You told this to Bollman? To whom else did you tell it?"

"To Thinwell, the man who drives me around and—"

"Fry me for an oyster!" Bertha exclaimed, jumping to her feet.

"What's the matter?" Kosling asked.

"Of all the numskulls, of all the thick-pated Dumb Doras!"

"Who?"

"Me."

"I don't get it," Kosling said.

"Any label on that music box, any place that would indicate the dealer, anything that—"

"I wouldn't know," Kosling said. "I am familiar with its appearance only through the sense of touch. It's strange, you asking who else I'd told about being afraid Josephine Dell had lost her memory because of that accident. I remember now Jerry Bollman asked me that same question."

"You told him you'd talked with Thinwell?"

"Yes. I have a doctor friend and Thinwell suggested I take him and go to see Miss Dell personally and ask her questions without letting on that the man with me was a doctor—but first, I should make absolutely certain that she was the one who had sent me that music box. Thinwell said that it just *might* have been someone else. But I don't see how it could have been. No, I'd never told anyone else about—"

"There was no note with the music box?" Bertha asked.

"No. The note was with the flowers. The music box was just delivered like I said, without any note."

Bertha started excitedly for the door, caught herself, turned back, stretched, yawned deliberately, and said, "Well, after all, I guess you've gone over things until you're tired. What do you say we turn in?"

"Wasn't there something in what I just said, something that made you excited?"

"Oh, I thought there was for a while," Bertha said, yawning again, "but I guess it's all a false alarm. Don't know what she paid for the music box, do you?"

"No, I don't, but I think it was rather a large sum. It's a very beautiful piece, and there's painting on it. Some kind of landscape painting done in oils."

"Ever had that painting described to you?"

"No, I've just felt it with my fingers."

Bertha sucked in another prodigious yawn.

"Well, I'm going to sleep. Do you like to sleep late in the morning?"

"Well, yes."

"I don't usually get up before nine or nine-thirty," Bertha said. "That isn't too late for you, is it?"

"The way I feel now, I could sleep the clock around."

"Well, go ahead and get a good night's sleep," Bertha told him. "I'll see you in the morning."

Bertha guided him through the door of the connecting bath, helped him off with the woman's clothes, piloted him around the room until he had the general lay of things, left his cane by his bed where he could reach it, and then said, "Well, sleep tight. I'll go grab some shut-eye."

She walked through the connecting bathroom, closed the door, listened for a moment, then grabbed her hat and coat, moved cautiously across the room, tiptoed down the corridor to the elevator, and ten minutes later was tearing madly along the road to Los Angeles.

It wasn't until she had passed Pomona that she suddenly realized she was doing exactly what Jerry Bollman had been doing some twenty-four hours previous—and probably for the same purpose. And now Jerry Bollman was stretched out on a slab.

Chapter Twenty-Six

DIM-OUT REGULATIONS were in effect. At the crest of the hill Bertha snapped her lights over to dim parking and crawled along at a conservative fifteen miles an hour. She swung her car in close to the curb, shut off the motor, and listened. She could hear nothing save the little night noises which had not as yet been frightened into silence—the chirping of crickets; the shrill chorus of frogs; and several other mysterious, unidentified noises of the night which are never heard near the more populous centers.

Bertha produced her pocket flashlight. By the aid of the weird, indistinct illumination, as intangible as pale moonlight, she found her way up the walk to the house.

The bungalow loomed suddenly before her, a dark silhouette. She followed the walk with the guide rail running along it, came to the porch, climbed the steps, and paused. The door was tightly closed. This would be the work of the officers. Bertha wondered whether it had been locked.

She tried the knob. The door was locked.

Bertha's flashlight showed her, after some difficulty in getting it properly centered, that there was no key on the inside of the door. The police then must either have put on a night latch or have closed and locked the door.

Bertha had a bunch of skeleton keys in her purse. She knew they constituted a dangerous possession, but they frequently came in very handy, and Bertha was not one to hesitate over something she wanted badly enough.

A skeleton key clicked in the lock. She tried three in succession. It was the fourth that unlatched the door.

Bertha Cool pushed the door open, then stood perfectly still, waiting to see if the dark interior of the house offered anything of menace.

She heard no sound. Her flashlight showed her nothing, although she mechanically depressed the beam over toward the left-hand corner in order to see if the sinister red stains were still on the carpet. They were.

Bertha switched out the flashlight.

Abruptly she heard motion in the room. Her ice-cold thumb fumbled with the switch of the flashlight. She was conscious of something coming toward her; then bony fingers seemed to clutch her throat.

Bertha lashed out in front of her with a frenzied kick. She swung her left fist and groped with her right, trying to find the wrists of her assailant.

Her hands encountered nothing. Her kick merely threw her off balance. She knew she had given a half-scream.

It wasn't until Bertha Cool had screamed that reason reinstated itself. The object at her throat abruptly left. She heard a fluttering sound, and caught the dim glimpse of a sinister shape flitting past her into the darkness.

"Freddie!" she muttered under her breath. "It's that damn bat."

She turned, the beam of her flashlight exploring the room while Bertha tried to convince herself there were no more death traps planted in the house against the return of the blind man.

Bertha's search of the place was necessarily impeded because of her desire to feel her way cautiously, to avoid running into some thread which, all but invisible in the dim light, would release a deadly bullet.

It was easy now to visualize what had happened the

night before; Bollman, hurrying into the house, trying to get that music box and get out before anyone caught him—the lunge against the string that led to the trap gun. Bertha, too, felt impelled by that same haste, that fear of discovery, yet she dared not surrender to it.

The house was plainly but comfortably furnished. Evidently Kosling tried to keep five or six comfortable chairs for his cronies when they came to visit. These chairs, all cushioned and comfortable, were arranged in a half-circle around the living-room. Against the wall under a window was a bookcase whose glass-enclosed shelves held no books, a table which was absolutely devoid of a magazine. On a stand over near the window— Bertha's eyes fixed on that stand. She advanced toward it. Her eager hands pounced upon the music box. When she had first seen it, when the blind man had exhibited it to her on the street, her inspection had been only casual. Now she studied it with a concentration that was all but microscopic.

The light of her flash showed Bertha that it was made of smoothly polished hardwood. On the outside was an oil painting of a pastoral scene. On the opposite side was a portrait of a beautiful young woman, somewhat ample so far as curves were judged by present-day standards, but quite definitely the belle of a bygone era.

At one time the paint had been varnished over, but now there were places where paint and varnish had worn thin. However, the grain of the wood showed through a beautiful satinlike finish, and the excellent preservation of the box indicated that here was something that had been long treasured as a family heirloom, something which had had the best of care. Little wonder that it had become one of the prized possessions of the affluent blind beggar.

Bertha explored the outside of it carefully, holding her spotlight within a couple of inches of the surface. There was not so much as a mark or a label on it. Disappointed, Bertha raised the cover. Almost instantly the music box picked up the strains of "Bluebells of Scotland" and filled the room with its tinkling sweetness.

Just inside the cover Bertha found what she wanted. A small oval label had been pasted on the top. It said, "Britten G. Stellman, Rare Antiques."

Bertha replaced the music box. The closing cover shut off the strains of music. She turned, started for the door, then came back to wipe her fingerprints from the music box.

Her spotlight turned toward the door. Vague, dancing blotches of darkness drifted along the wall, looking as though dark figures were bunched there waiting to pounce on her. Bertha realized that it was the bat flying in frenzied circles around the room, casting shadows when it crossed the beam of her spotlight. Evidently the bat was hungry for human companionship, but sensed that Bertha was not the blind man.

Bertha tried to entice the bat outside so that she could close the door, but the bat apparently preferred to stay inside.

Bertha made little "cheeping" noises, finally said in exasperation, "Come on, Freddie, you old fool. Get out of here. I'm going to close and lock that door. You'll die if I leave you inside."

It might have been that the bat understood her, or perhaps the sound of the human voice sent him once more fluttering around her head.

"Get away," Bertha said, brushing at him with her hand. "You make me nervous, and if you get on my neck again, I'll—"

"Exactly what *will* you do, Mrs. Cool?" the voice of Sergeant Sellers asked. "You have me definitely interested now."

Bertha jumped as though she had been jabbed with a pin, turned around, and at first failed to locate the sergeant's hiding-place. Then she saw him standing by a vine-covered corner of the porch, his hands resting on the rail, his chin on the backs of his hands. Standing on the ground, he was some two feet lower than Bertha Cool, and Bertha, looking down at him, could sense the triumph on the man's smiling countenance.

"All right," Bertha snapped. "Go ahead and say it."

"Burglary," Sergeant Sellers observed, "is a very serious crime."

"This isn't burglary," Bertha snapped.

"Indeed? Perhaps you've had a special act passed by the legislature, or the Supreme Court may have changed the law, but a breaking and entering such as you have just done—"

"It's just a little trick of the law that you don't happen to know," Bertha said. "To make it burglary, you must break and enter for the purpose of committing grand or petit larceny or some felony."

Sellers thought that over for a minute, then laughed and said, "By George, I believe you *are* right."

"I know I'm right," Bertha snapped. "I wasn't associated with the best legal brain in the country for several years for nothing."

"That brings up a very interesting question. Exactly what *was* your purpose in entering the house?"

Bertha, doing some fast thinking, said triumphantly, "I had to let the bat out."

"Ah, yes, the bat," Sergeant Sellers said. "I'll admit it eluded me. You gave it a name, I believe. Freddie, wasn't it?"

"That's right."

"Most interesting. That's the tame bat?"

"Yes."

"More and more interesting. And you came here to let it out?"

"Yes."

"Why?"

"I knew that it would die for lack of food and water if someone didn't let it out."

Sergeant Sellers came walking around the corner of the porch to climb up the stairs and stand on a level with Bertha Cool. "I'm not trying to be funny. I'm trying to be polite. You might also remember that I'm asking these questions not as a mere matter of idle curiosity, but in my official capacity."

"I know," Bertha said. "You're putting on a lot of dog, but you're boring in just the same. I always did distrust a polysyllabic cop."

Sellers laughed.

Bertha said, "When they started putting college men on the force, they damn near ruined it."

"Oh, come, Mrs. Cool. It isn't as bad as that."

"It's worse."

"Well, let's not discuss the police force in the abstract at the moment. I'm interested in bats—and one bat in particular, Freddie."

"All right, what about Freddie? I've told you why I came out here."

"You wanted to release Freddie. You knew he was in the building then."

"I thought he might be."

"What gave you that idea?"

"Kosling had it so the bat could get in and out. He always left the door open a few inches and blocked it with a rubber wedge so it wouldn't blow either open or shut. I kept thinking that perhaps you men had been dumb enough to shut the door and leave the bat locked inside."

"I'm quite certain we didn't, Mrs. Cool. I think the bat came in from the outside."

"Yes, I suppose so."

"And gave you quite a start. You screamed and—"

"Well, it would give you a start, too, if something came out of the night and perched on your chest."

"The bat did that?"

"Yes."

"Very interesting. Do you know, Mrs. Cool, I think this is the first time I've ever had a case which involved a pet bat? I think it's the first time I've ever heard of a person making a pet out of a bat."

"You're young yet."

"Thank you."

"And how did you happen to be sitting out here waiting for me to come and let the bat loose?" Bertha asked.

He said, "That is indeed a coincidence. More and more I've been wondering whether we had the correct theory of what happened last night. I thought that it might—just barely *might* be possible that your friend, Jerry Bollman, pumped your blind client, received some very interesting information which made him feel there was something the blind man had that he wanted. In place of coming out here with Kosling, he left Kosling somewhere and came out here alone to get the thing he wanted. Obviously, he didn't get it. If he *did* get it, he certainly didn't carry it away with him; but the indications are he walked into that deadly trap gun and was killed as soon as he entered the place. A snare gun that was rigged up by a blind man for a blind victim. Most interesting. We've heard of the blind leading the blind, but this is a case where the blind kill the blind."

"Go right ahead," Bertha said. "Don't mind me. I've got lots of time."

"Then," Sergeant Sellers went on, "it began to dawn on me that perhaps I had been just a bit credulous. When I was in your office this afternoon, a collect telephone call came through."

"Was there anything remarkable about that?" Bertha Cool snapped. "Didn't you ever have anyone call you collect on long-distance?"

Sellers's triumphant grin showed that she had led with her chin. "The remarkable thing, Mrs. Cool, was that you accepted the call after you found out who was calling —and then a very peculiar circumstance popped into my mind. After you hung up the telephone, there was some more talk about Rodney Kosling. You didn't say that you didn't know where he was *after* you had hung up the telephone, but you did use a rather peculiar sentence construction. You said that you had answered all of my questions truthfully, according to the best information you had at the time.

"I'll admit, Mrs. Cool, I didn't think of it until after dinner; then it dawned on me as an interesting possibility. I didn't want to lose face among my subordinates by staking any of them out here, in case it proved to be a poor hunch, and I didn't want to trust the examination to anyone else, in case it proved to be a good one. But it was an interesting possibility. Suppose Bollman came out here for something. Suppose you went to meet Rodney Kosling. Suppose you found out what it was Bollman had come out here to get, and suppose *you* came out and picked up that particular article. That would be very, very interesting."

Bertha said, "I didn't take a thing from that house."

"That, of course, is an assertion which will have to be checked," Sellers said. "Much as I dislike to do so, Mrs. Cool, I'm going to have to ask you to get in my automobile and go to headquarters where a matron will search you. If it turns out you haven't taken anything, then—well, then, of course, the situation will be radically different. If it should appear that you *have* taken something, then, of course, you'd be guilty of a crime, the crime of burglary. And, as a person apprehended in the act of committing a burglary, we'd have to hold you, Mrs. Cool. We'd have to hold you at least until we had a very fair, full, and frank statement of just *what* you're trying to do."

Bertha said, "You can't do this to me. You can't—"

"Indeed, I can," Sellers said, quite affably. "I'm doing it. If you *haven't* taken anything out of the building, I suppose I can't make a burglary charge stick, unless, as you so competently point out, I could prove that you entered the building for the purpose of committing a felony in the first place. Looks almost as though you had looked up the law before you made your visit."

"Well, I didn't."

"That, of course, is another statement of fact which is open to investigation, although I don't know just how we're going to prove it. But in any event, Mrs. Cool, I'm placing you under arrest, and I think, as a student of law, you understand that if you now do anything to interfere, you will be resisting arrest, which, in itself, is a crime."

Bertha Cool thought that over, looked at Sergeant

Sellers, recognized the inflexibility of purpose behind his smiling mask, and said, "Okay, you win."

"We'll just leave your car parked right where it is," Sellers said. "I wouldn't want you to dispose of anything between here and headquarters—and since the tinkling melody of the 'Bluebells of Scotland' shows me that you went to the music box and raised the lid, it is quite evident that the object you took from the music box was relatively small and, therefore, something that could be easily concealed. So, Mrs. Cool, if you wouldn't mind going into the room again so I can keep my eye on you while I pick up that music box, we'll take it right along to headquarters with us."

"All right, you've got me," Bertha Cool said. "Go ahead. Rub it in! Go on and gloat!"

"No gloating at all, Mrs. Cool, just a slight formality. Now, then, if you'll walk just ahead of me, and if you wouldn't mind keeping your hands up where I can see them. That spotlight of yours isn't very efficient. I think you'll find mine a lot better."

Sergeant Sellers's five-cell flashlight blazed into brilliance, lighting the way into the front room of the little bungalow.

Chapter Twenty-Seven

THE MATRON escorted Bertha Cool to the door of Sergeant Sellers's private office and knocked.

The tinkling strains of "Bluebells of Scotland" sounded faintly through the door.

"Come in," Sellers called.

The matron opened the door. "In this way, *dearie*," she said to Bertha Cool.

Bertha paused on the threshold, turned, looked at the matron—two, husky, bulldog-jawed women glaring at each other. "All right, *dearie*," Bertha Cool said.

"What did you find?" Sergeant Sellers inquired.

"Nothing," the matron announced.

Sergeant Sellers raised his eyebrows. "Well, well. Don't

tell me that you went there just for the experience, Mrs. Cool?"

"You forget Freddie," Bertha said. "Got a cigarette? Your girl friend snitched my package."

"Oh, I'm sorry. I forgot your cigarettes," the matron said. "I put them up on that—"

"It's all right, *dearie*. Keep them with my compliments," Bertha said.

The matron caught Sergeant Sellers's eye and seemed embarrassed. "You should have said something about them at the time, Mrs. Cool."

"I didn't know I was supposed to," Bertha announced. "I thought it was a privilege that went with the office, like the cops taking apples from the fruit stands."

"That's all, Mrs. Bell," Sergeant Sellers said.

The matron glared at Bertha Cool, then quietly withdrew.

"Sit down," Sellers said to Bertha Cool. "Let's see, you wanted a cigarette. Here's one."

He opened a fresh package of cigarettes, and handed Bertha one. He fished a black, moist cigar from his waistcoat pocket, clipped off the end, shoved it in his mouth, and, for the moment, made no effort to light it.

"Something about this music box," he said.

"Indeed?"

"You went to it, opened it, then closed it and left. You didn't take anything out. I wonder if you put something *in*."

Sellers took a magnifying glass from his drawer, went over the music box carefully, inspecting both the works and the case, looking for some place of concealment which might harbor some bit of planted evidence. When he could find none, he closed the music box, studied the outside of it, and looked at the portrait of the young woman. "I wonder if *this* is it?"

"What?"

"The portrait. It isn't a missing heiress, is it?"

Bertha, feeling remarkably good after winning her verbal encounter with the matron, settled back in her chair and laughed.

"Why the laughter?"

"Thinking of the nineteenth-century beauty," Bertha said. "A chunky, mealymouthed nincompoop who wore corsets and fainted at the faintest suggestion of salty humor. And you think I'd go all the way from—"

"Yes, yes," Sergeant Sellers said as Bertha stopped. "You interest me now. All the way from where, Mrs. Cool?"

Bertha clamped her lips tightly shut.

"Almost told me something, didn't you?" Sergeant Sellers said.

Bertha, realizing how close she had come to saying, "All the way from Riverside," contented herself with puffing placidly away at her cigarette, atoning for what was almost a verbal slip by maintaining a rigid silence.

Sergeant Sellers looked at the big clock over the desk. "Ten minutes past two," he mused. "It's rather late, but then—this probably is an emergency."

He consulted the label on the inside of the music box, studied a telephone directory, then picked up the receiver, said, "Give me an outside line," and dialed a number.

After a few moments, he said suavely, "I'm very sorry about having to call you at this hour. This is Sergeant Sellers speaking from police headquarters, and the reason I'm calling is because I'm trying to trace an important clue in a murder case. Is this Britton G. Stellman? It is, eh? Well, I want you to tell me whether you can remember a music box, one of the old-fashioned kind with a metal comb and a cylinder—has a picture of a landscape on one side and the portrait of a girl on the other, plays 'Bluebells of Scotland,' and—oh, I see—you do, eh? Yes. What was her name? Josephine Dell, eh?"

Sergeant Sellers was silent for several seconds, listening to the voice which came over the telephone; then he said, "All right, now let me see if I've got this straight. This Josephine Dell came in about a month ago, saw this music box, and said she'd like to get it but didn't have enough money to pay for it. She left a small deposit to hold it for ninety days. Then she rang you up on Wednesday, told you she had the money available, and that she was sending it to you by telegram. She asked you to deliver the music box by messenger to this blind man without saying anything about who sent it; just to tell him that it was a present from a friend—that right?"

Again Sellers was silent for several moments while he was listening; then he said, "Okay. One more question. Where was that telegram sent from? Redlands, eh? You don't know whether she lives in Redlands? Oh, I see. Lives in Los Angeles and you think she just happened to be traveling through Redlands. You don't think that she's any relation to this blind man, didn't say anything about that? Just saw her the one time when she was in and paid the deposit, eh? Say where she was working? I see. All right, thanks a lot. I wouldn't have called you at this hour if it hadn't been a major emergency. I can assure you your co-operation is appreciated. Yes, this is Sergeant Sellers of Homicide. I'll drop in and see you next time I'm in the neighborhood and thank you personally. In the meantime, if anything turns up, give me a ring. All right, thanks. Good-by."

Sergeant Sellers hung up the telephone, turned to Bertha Cool, and looked her over as though he were seeing her for the first time.

"Rather cute," he said.

"I don't get it."

Sergeant Sellers said, "I am just wondering, Mrs. Cool, if that collect telephone call you received this afternoon didn't come from Redlands."

"It certainly did not," Bertha assured him.

"You'll pardon me if I make a little investigation of that."

"Go ahead. Investigate all you want to."

"I don't think you understand me, Mrs. Cool. During the investigation I am going to make, it's going to be necessary for me to have you where I can find you."

"What do you mean by that?"

"I mean exactly what I say."

"You mean you're going to put me under surveillance?"

"Oh, that would be an unnecessary expense to the city, Mrs. Cool. I wouldn't think of doing anything like that. And besides, it would inconvenience you so much."

"Well, what *do* you mean then?"

"If you were traveling around, going here and there, wherever you wanted to go, it would cause us a lot of trouble to keep track of you; but if you stayed in one place, it wouldn't be at all difficult."

"You mean my office?"

"Or mine."

"Just what *do* you mean?"

"Well, I thought that if you stayed here for a while it might simplify matters."

"You can't hold me in custody that way."

"Certainly not," Sellers said. "I would be the first one to admit that, Mrs. Cool."

"Well," she said triumphantly.

"Just a moment," he cautioned as she started to get up out of the chair. "I can't hold you on *that*, but I certainly can hold you on breaking into the house tonight. That's a felony."

"But I didn't take anything."

"We can't be entirely certain of that as yet."

"I've been searched."

"But you *might* have managed to get rid of whatever you had taken, or you might have been *intending* to commit a felony. Do you know, Mrs. Cool, I think I'll hold you a little while longer on that charge, and there are a couple of other things I'd like to look up."

"Such as what?" Bertha demanded indignantly.

"Well, for instance, the way you left your office this afternoon. You went down and took a streetcar on Seventh Street. You got out just above Grand Avenue. My two plain-clothes men who were following you thought they had a cinch. You were on foot, apparently depending on streetcars. The man who was driving the car dropped the detective who was with him, and drove around the block so he could come back and slide in at a space opposite a fire plug which he'd spotted as he drove down the street just before you got off the streetcar. And then your automobile came along and picked you up and whisked you away just as neatly as though you'd been engineering a sleight-of-hand trick."

Sergeant Sellers pressed the bell which summoned the matron. When she arrived in the office he said, "Mrs. Bell, Mrs. Cool is going to be with us, at least until morning. Will you try to make her comfortable?"

The matron's smile held the triumph of cold malice. "It will be a pleasure, Sergeant," she said, and then, turning belligerently to Bertha: "Come with me, *dearie*."

Chapter Twenty-Eight

SLOW, METHODICAL STEPS echoed down the steel-lined corridor. Bertha Cool, sitting in seething indignation on the edge of an iron cot, heard the clank of keys, then the sound of a key in the door just outside. A moment later, the door came open, and a rather drab-looking woman said, "Hello," in a lifeless voice.

"Who are you?" Bertha asked.

"I'm a trusty."

"What do you want?"

"They want you down in the office."

"What for?"

"That's all I know."

"Well, to hell with them. I'm staying here."

"I wouldn't do that if I were you."

"Why not?"

"It won't get you any place."

"Let them come and take me," Bertha said.

"Don't kid yourself. They can do that, too. But I'd go along if I was you. I think they're going to turn you loose."

"Well, I'll stay right here."

"For how long?"

163

"From now on."

"That won't do you no good. Lots of them feel that way, but you don't hurt nobody by staying here. You've got to go *some*time, and then they have the laugh on you." The trusty spoke in the same dejected, flat monotone with a leisurely drawl, as though the effort of speaking wearied her and consumed too much vitality. "I remember one woman said she was going to stay here, and they told me just to leave the door unlocked and tell her she could go whenever she wanted to. She stayed there all morning. It was the middle of the afternoon when she finally went out, and everybody gave her the ha-ha."

Bertha, without a word, got up from the cot and followed the trusty down the echoing corridor, through a locked door into an elevator, down to an office where another matron who was a stranger to Bertha looked up from some papers and said, "Is this Bertha Cool?"

"This is Bertha Cool, and you'd better take a good look at me because you're going to see more of me. I'm going to—"

The matron opened a drawer, pulled out a heavy, sealed Manila envelope and said, "These are your personal belongings which were taken from you when you were put in last night, Mrs. Cool. Will you please look them over and see if they're all there?"

"I'm going to take this damn place apart," Bertha said. "You can't do anything like that to me. I'm a respectable woman making a decent, honest living, and—"

"But, in the meantime, will you please check your personal belongings?"

"I'm going to sue the city, and I'm going to sue Sergeant Sellers. I—"

"I know, Mrs. Cool. Doubtless you are. But that's outside of my department. If you'll please check your personal property—"

"Well, you may think it's outside of your department, but, by the time I get done, you'll find out it isn't outside of anybody's department. I'll—"

"When did you intend to start this suit, Mrs. Cool?"

"Just as soon as I can get to see a lawyer."

"And you can't get a lawyer until you get out, and you can't get out until you check your personal property, so please check your personal property."

Bertha Cool ripped open the envelope, pulled out her purse, opened it with rage-trembling hands, glanced through it, snapped it shut, and said, "So what?"

The matron nodded to the trusty.

"This way, ma'am."

Bertha Cool stood over the desk. "I've heard of lots of outrages being perpetrated on citizens, but this is—"

"You were held on suspicion of burglary last night, Mrs. Cool. I don't think that any disposition has been made of the charge, but the order came through to release you pending a further investigation."

"Oh, I see," Bertha said. "You're threatening me now. If I start anything, you're going to bring up that burglary charge, are you? I—"

"I don't know anything at all about it, Mrs. Cool. I'm simply telling you the state of the record. It's our custom to do that with persons who are held on suspicion of crime. Good morning, Mrs. Cool."

Bertha still stood there. "I'm a businesswoman. I have important things to do in connection with running my business. Taking me away from my work, holding me all night on a trumped-up charge—"

"Your time's valuable?"

"Certainly."

"I wouldn't waste any more of it standing here then, Mrs. Cool."

Bertha said, "I'm not going to. I just want to leave you a message for Sergeant Sellers. Tell him that his threat didn't work, will you. Tell him that I'm going to have his scalp, and now, GOOD MORNING!"

Bertha Cool turned toward the door.

"Just one more thing, Mrs. Cool."

"What is it?" Bertha demanded.

"You can't slam the door," the matron said. "We've put an automatic check on it for that particular purpose.

165

Good morning."

Bertha found herself ushered out of a steel-barred door into the morning sunlight, just as though she had been some ordinary criminal. She found also that the fresh air, the freedom of motion, the feeling that she was able to go as she pleased, when she pleased, and how she pleased, was a more welcome sensation than she had ever realized.

It was eight forty-five when she got to her office.

Elsie Brand was opening the mail.

Bertha, storming into the office, slammed her purse down on the table, and said in a voice quivering with indignation, "You get me Sergeant Sellers on the line, Elsie. I don't give a damn if you have to get him out of bed or what happens, you get Sergeant Sellers for me."

Elsie Brand, looking at Bertha's quivering, white-raged indignation, dropped the mail, grabbed the telephone directory, and immediately started putting through the call.

"Hello, police headquarters? I want to talk with Sergeant Sellers immediately, please. It's important. Yes. Bertha Cool's office. Just a moment, Sergeant. Here he is on the line, Mrs. Cool."

Bertha Cool grabbed up the telephone. "I've got something to say to you," she said. "I've had a long time to think it over—a good long time, sitting in your damned jail. I just want to tell you that I'm going to—"

"Don't," Sergeant Sellers interrupted, laughing.

Bertha said, "I'm going to—"

"You're going to cool down," Sellers interrupted again, the laughter suddenly gone from his voice. "You used to run a fairly average detective agency; then you got tied up with this streak of dynamite, Donald Lam, and you started cutting corners. You've cut corners in every case you've had. Because Lam is a whiz, you've been able to get away with it. But now you're out on your own, and you've stubbed your toe. You've been caught breaking into a house. All the police have to do is to press that charge against you, and you'd lose your license and—"

"Don't think you can intimidate me, you great big

bum," Bertha Cool shouted. "I wish I were a man just long enough to come up there and pull you out of your office chair and pin your ears back. I know now how people can get mad enough to commit murder. I just wish I had you where I could get my hands on you. Why, you—"

Bertha choked with sheer inarticulate rage.

Sergeant Sellers said, "I'm sorry you feel that way about it, Mrs. Cool, but I thought it was necessary to keep you shut up overnight while I made a few investigations. It may interest you to know that as a result of those investigations we've made substantial progress toward cleaning up the case."

"I don't give a damn what you've done," Bertha said.

"And," Sellers went on, "in case you're in a hurry to go back to Riverside and pick up your aged mother who's had a stroke, Mrs. Cool, you can save yourself the trouble, because your *mother* is here in my office at the present time. I'm having him make an affidavit as to what happened. After the district attorney sees that affidavit, you may have another interval of incarceration. I think you'll find in the long run it pays to be law-abiding and to co-operate with the police. And, by the way, we picked up your automobile and drove it back to the garage where you store it. After searching it, of course. The next time you want to go anywhere, I'd suggest you just go to the garage and drive out in your car. Not that it's any of *my* business, but your juggling around with streetcars and automobiles will convince a grand jury that you *intended* to commit some crime when you started for San Bernardino yesterday. That's rather bad, you know. Good-by."

Sergeant Sellers dropped the receiver into place at the other end of the line.

Flabbergasted, Bertha Cool made two abortive attempts to get the receiver in its cradle before she finally succeeded.

"What is it?" Elsie Brand asked, looking at her face.

Bertha's rage was gone now. An emotional reaction left

her white and shaken. "I'm in a jam," she said, and walked over to the nearest chair and sat down.

"What's the matter?"

"I went out and got that blind man. I smuggled him out of the hotel. I was absolutely satisfied the police would never trace me. I stubbed my toe. Now, they've got him—and they've got me. That damn, overbearing, bullying, sneering police sergeant is right. They've got me over a barrel."

"That bad?" Elsie Brand asked.

"It's worse," Bertha Cool said. "Well, there's no use in stopping now. You've got to keep on moving. It's like skating near the center of a pond where the ice begins to buckle. The minute you stop, you're finished. You've just *got* to keep moving."

"Where to?" Elsie asked.

"Right now, to Redlands."

"Why Redlands?" Elsie Brand asked. "I don't get it."

Bertha told her about the music box, the conversation Sergeant Sellers had had with the owner, and with a sudden unusual burst of confidence, the entire adventures of the night.

"Well," Bertha Cool said at length, heaving herself up out of the chair, "I didn't sleep a damn wink last night. I was just too mad. I never regretted taking off weight as much in my life as I did last night."

"Why?" Elsie asked.

"Why!" Bertha exclaimed. "I'll tell you why. There was a damn snooty matron who kept calling me *dearie*. She was a husky, broad-shouldered biddy, but before I took off my weight, I could have thrown her down and sat on her. And that's exactly what I'd have done. I'd have sat on her and stayed there the whole blessed night. I'm in a jam, Elsie. I've got to get out of the office and lay low until the thing blows over. They've got that blind man, and he'll tell them the whole business. Sergeant Sellers was right. I should have kept on doing business in the routine way. But Donald is such a reckless little runt, and he did such daring damn things, he got me into bad habits. I got to thinking, Elsie. I'm going out of here and get a drink of whisky—and then I'm going to Redlands."

Chapter Twenty-Nine

HOT, DRY SUNLIGHT beat down on Redlands. The dark green of orange groves laid out in neat checkerboards contrasted with the deep blue of the clear sky and the towering peaks which rose more than ten thousand feet above sea level in the background. There was a clean, washed freshness about the dry air which should have been invigorating, but Bertha's worry and preoccupation made her entirely oblivious of the beauty of the scenery and the freshness of the air.

Bertha dragged herself out of the automobile, plowed across the sidewalk, head down, arms swinging, climbed the steps of the sanitarium, entered the lobby, and said in a flat, dejected voice to the girl at the information desk, "Do you, by any chance, have a Josephine Dell here?"

"Just a moment." The girl thumbed through a card index, said, "Yes. She has a private room, two-o-seven."

"A nurse there?" Bertha asked.

"No. Apparently she's just here for a complete rest."

Bertha said, "Thank you," and went pounding her weary way down the long corridor. She found the elevator, went to the second floor, found room 207, knocked gently on the swinging door and pushed it open.

A blond girl about twenty-seven with deep-blue eyes, smiling lips, and a slightly upturned nose, sat in a chair by the window. She was attired in a silk negligee. Her ankles were crossed on a pillow placed on another chair in front of her. She was reading a book with every evidence of enjoyment, but looked up with a start as Bertha entered the room, letting Bertha have the benefit of the large, deep-blue eyes.

"You startled me."

"I knocked," Bertha explained.

ERLE STANLEY GARDNER

"I was interested in this detective story. Do you ever read them?"

"Once in a while," Bertha said.

"I never have until I came to the hospital. I didn't think I'd ever have the time, but now I'm going to become an ardent fan. I think the detection of crime is the most absorbing, the most interesting thing in the world, don't you?"

Bertha said, "It's all in the way you look at it, I guess."

"Well, do sit down. Tell me what I can do for you."

Bertha Cool dropped wearily into the cushioned chair over in the corner. "You're Josephine Dell?"

"Yes."

"And *you're* the one who is friendly with the blind man?"

"Oh, you mean that blind man on the corner by the bank building?" the girl asked eagerly.

Bertha nodded dispiritedly.

"I think he's a dear. I think he's one of the nicest men I've ever known. He has the most sane outlook on life. He isn't soured at all. Lots of people who are blind would shut themselves off from the world, but he doesn't. He seems to be more aware of the world now that he's blind than he possibly could have been when he had his eyesight. And I think he's really happy, although, of course, his existence is very much circumscribed. That is, I mean physically and so far as contacts are concerned."

"I suppose so," Bertha admitted, without enthusiasm.

Josephine Dell warmed to her subject. "Of course, the man was relatively uneducated and poor to start with. If he had only learned to read by touch, had started studying and given himself an education—but he couldn't do it. He simply couldn't afford to. He was absolutely penniless and destitute."

"I understand."

"Then he got lucky. He made a very fortunate investment in oil, and now he can live very much as he pleases; but he feels that it's too late, that he's too old."

170

"I suppose so," Bertha agreed. "You're the one who sent him the music box?"

"Yes—but I didn't want him to know that. I just wanted it to come to him from a friend. I was afraid he wouldn't accept that expensive a gift from a working girl, although I can afford it now very well. At the time I started paying for it, I felt that I couldn't."

"I see," Bertha said wearily. "Well, I seem to have been whipsawed all the way around. I don't suppose you happen to know anything about the Josephine Dell who had the accident, do you?"

"What accident?" she asked curiously.

Bertha said, "The accident that took place there on the corner by the bank building about quarter to six Friday night. The man hit this young woman with his automobile and knocked her down. She didn't think she was hurt much, but—"

"But *I'm* that person," Josephine Dell said.

The sag snapped out of Bertha Cool's back as she jerked herself rigidly erect. "You're what?" she asked.

"I'm that girl."

"One of us," Bertha announced, "is nuts."

Josephine Dell laughed, a musical, tinkling bit of laughter. "Oh, but I am. It was the most peculiar experience. This man struck me and knocked me down, and he seemed like a very nice young man. I didn't think I was hurt at the time, and the next morning when I got up, I began to be a little dizzy and had a headache. I called a doctor, and the doctor said it looked like concussion. He advised a complete rest and—"

"Wait a minute," Bertha said. "Did this man drive you home?"

"He wanted to, and I decided to let him. At the time I didn't think I was hurt at all. I just thought I'd been knocked over, and I felt a little sheepish about it, because—well, after all, while I was in the right, so far as the signal was concerned, I really wasn't watching where I was going. I had some things on my mind that day, and—well, anyway, he insisted that I must go to a hospital for a check-up; and when I refused that, he said he was going to drive me home, anyway."

Bertha Cool looked as though she were seeing ghosts. "What happened?"

"Well, the man seemed like very much of a gentleman, but I hadn't been riding with him very long before I realized he had been drinking. Then I saw he was quite intoxicated, and then the veneer of being a gentleman wore through. He started making offensive remarks, and finally started pawing. I slapped his face, got out of the car, and took a streetcar home."

"You hadn't told him where you lived?"

"No, just the direction to start driving."

"And he didn't have your name?"

"I gave it to him, but he was too drunk to remember it. I'm absolutely certain of that."

Bertha did everything but rub her eyes. "Now," she said, "all you need to do to make the thing completely cockeyed is to tell me that you were living in the Bluebonnet Apartments."

"But I was—I still am. The Bluebonnet Apartments out on Figueroa. How did you know?"

Bertha Cool put her hand to her head.

"What's the matter?" Josephine Dell asked.

"Fry me for an oyster," Bertha said, "pickle me for a herring, and can me for a sardine. I'm a poor fish."

"But I don't understand."

"Just go ahead. Tell me the rest of it."

"Well that's about all there is to it. I got up the next morning and felt dizzy. I called the doctor and he suggested I should take a complete rest. I didn't have any money on hand, but I had a little money coming. I thought that perhaps I could arrange something so I could— Well, I knew that Mrs. Cranning, the housekeeper, had a housekeeping fund from which she paid bills; and I thought perhaps I could get a little salary advance on that. I suppose I should tell you the man I was working for had died rather suddenly—"

"I know all about that," Bertha said. "Tell me about

the money angle."

"Well, I went to Mrs. Cranning, and she didn't have enough to spare to enable me to do just what I wanted to do, but she told me to go in and lie down and she'd see what she could do. Well, she certainly did a splendid job. The insurance company made a perfectly splendid adjustment."

"And what did it do?"

"They agreed with my doctor that what I needed was a complete rest for a month or six weeks, and that I should go to some place where I wouldn't have a thing in the world to worry about, where I wouldn't have any of my old contacts or associations to bother me. My employer had died, and I was going to be out of a job, anyway. Well, the insurance company agreed to send me here, pay every cent of expenses, give me my salary for the two months I was here. When I left, they were to give me a check for five hundred dollars and guarantee to find me a job. Isn't that generous?"

"Did you sign anything?" Bertha asked.

"Oh, yes, a complete agreement—a release I guess it's called."

Bertha said, "Good God!"

"But I don't understand. Can't you tell me what's the matter? What I'm telling you seems to distress you."

"The insurance company," Bertha said, "was the Intermutual Indemnity Company, and the agent was P. L. Fosdick?"

"Why, no."

"Who was it?" Bertha Cool asked.

"It was an automobile club. I've forgotten the exact name of it, but I think it was the Auto Parity Club. I know the agent's name was Milbran. He's the one who made all the arrangements."

"How did you cash the check?" Bertha asked.

"The settlement was made in the form of cash, because it was on Saturday afternoon. The banks were closed, and Mr. Milbran thought I should come right out here where it was quiet. He said that he was making a generous settlement with me because of the circumstances. Do you know what he told me—after the agreement had been signed, of course?"

"No," Bertha said. "What?"

She laughed. "Said that his client was so drunk that he actually didn't know he had hit anyone. He admitted that he'd been drinking heavily and was driving the car home; but he doesn't even remember having been in that particular section of the city where he hit me, and certainly doesn't remember the accident. It came as a shock to him when—"

"Wait a minute," Bertha Cool interrupted. "How did you get in touch with the insurance company then?"

"That was through Mrs. Cranning."

"I know, but how did she get in touch with it? What—"

"Well, I remembered this man's license number."

"Did you write it down?" Bertha asked.

"No, I didn't write it down. I just remembered it, and I told Mrs. Cranning what it was. Of course, I wrote it down after I got home. When I say I didn't write it down, I mean I didn't stand right there in front of the automobile and write it down. I didn't want to be disagreeable about the thing, but I just looked at his license number so as to— Why, what's the matter?"

Bertha Cool said, "You've done the damnedest thing."

"I have?"

"Yes."

"What? I don't understand."

"You got the license number wrong," Bertha Cool said, "and just as a pure coincidence your wrong license number happened to be that of a man who was also driving a car at that time and was also drunk."

"You mean that the man—that the Club—"

"That's exactly what I mean," Bertha said. "You got hold of a man who happened to have been too drunk at the time to know what he was doing but who realized he *might* have hit someone. When Mrs. Cranning got in touch with him and told him about the accident, he rang up his insurance carrier and reported to them, and the insurance carrier came dashing out to make the best settlement he could."

"And you mean this man didn't hit me at all?"

"Not the one you made the claim against."

"But that's impossible!"

"I know it's impossible," Bertha observed doggedly, "but it's exactly what happened."

"And where does that leave me?"

Bertha said, "It leaves you sitting on top of the world."

"I'm afraid I don't understand."

Bertha Cool opened her purse, pulled out one of her agency cards, and put on her best smile. "Here," she said, "is one of my cards. Cool & Lam, Confidential Investigators. I'm Bertha Cool."

"You mean—that you're a detective?"

"Yes."

"How exciting!"

"Not very."

"But don't you— Oh, you must have unusual experiences. You must work at odd hours, have sleepless nights—"

"Yes," Bertha interrupted, "we have unusual experiences and sleepless nights. I had an unusual experience yesterday and a particularly sleepless night. And now I've found *you*."

"But why were you looking for me?"

Bertha Cool said, "I am going to collect some money for you. Will you give me fifty per cent of it if I collect it?"

"Money for what?"

"Money from the insurance company for being hit by a drunken driver."

"But I've already collected that, Mrs. Cool. I've already made a settlement."

"No, you haven't, not from the man who was driving the car. How much were they going to pay in all?"

"You mean this insurance company?"

"Yes, the one you made the settlement with, this Auto Club outfit?"

175

"Why, they were going to pay me my salary for two months. That would be two hundred and fifty dollars for the two months. Then they were going to pay all the expenses here. I don't know what they amount to, but I think it's ten dollars a day. That would be six hundred dollars for two months, and give me five hundred dollars when I left here. Good heavens, Mrs. Cool, do you realize how much that is? That's thirteen hundred dollars."

"All right," Bertha said, "you signed a release, releasing the client of that insurance company, and that insurance company from any claim. You didn't sign any release, releasing the Intermutual Indemnity Company. Now, I'll tell you what we're going to do. You're going to put your claim in my hands, and I'm going to collect you a bunch of money from the Intermutual. You're going to pay me one half of what I collect, and I'm going to guarantee with you that your share will be at least two thousand dollars."

"You mean two thousand dollars in *cash?*"

"Yes," Bertha said. "That'll be *your* share, and don't let's have any misunderstandings, dear. I'll be making two thousand dollars myself. Understand, that's a minimum. I feel certain I can get you more, perhaps three or four thousand dollars as your share."

"But, Mrs. Cool, that would be dishonest."

"Why would it be dishonest?"

"Because I've already given a release to the insurance company."

"But it was the wrong insurance company, the wrong driver."

"I know, but, nevertheless, I've accepted that money."

"They've paid it to you," Bertha said. "It's their hard luck."

"No, I couldn't do that. It wouldn't be ethical. It wouldn't be honest."

"Listen," Bertha said, "the insurance companies have lots of money. They're rolling in wealth. This man was driving a car. He was so drunk he didn't know what he was doing. When Mrs. Cranning rang him up and told him that he'd hit you, knocked you down, and then made passes at you going home, he really thought he'd done so. He told her he'd have his insurance company get on the job right away. He called up his insurance company and said, 'I'm in an awful jam. I was driving a car last night. I was so drunk I don't know what happened, and I hit this girl. She's had a concussion of the brain and is lying on a couch out there at the house of the man who employed her. For God's sake, get on the job quick and clean the thing up.' "

"Well?" Josephine Dell asked. "Suppose he did?"

"Don't you see what happened? He didn't hit you at all, and because you gave them a release, it doesn't mean a thing. In other words, if I should be ninny enough to offer a thousand dollars for a complete release of any and all claims you might have against me, because I hit you with an automobile, it wouldn't prevent you from collecting from someone who *did* hit you with an automobile."

A frown puckered the smooth skin of Josephine Dell's forehead. Her blond hair glinted in the sunlight as she turned her head to look out of the window while she studied the proposition. Then, at length, she gave Bertha Cool her answer, a firm, determined shake of the head.

"No, Mrs. Cool, I couldn't do it. It wouldn't be fair."

"Then," Bertha said, "if you want to be absolutely fair, ring up this automobile club representative and tell him that it was all a mistake, that you got the license number wrong."

Instant suspicion appeared in Josephine Dell's eyes. "I don't think I got the license number wrong," she said.

"I tell you, you did."

"How do you know?"

"Because I know the insurance company that's actually handling the case."

"All right," Josephine Dell said, "if you know so much about it, go ahead and tell me what was wrong with the license number. What was the license number of the man who *did* hit me?"

Bertha Cool tried to avoid that. She said, "I've actually talked with the representative of the insurance company. He told me that if you—"

"What was the license number of the man who *did* hit me?" Josephine Dell interrupted.

"I don't know," Bertha Cool confessed.

"I thought not," Josephine Dell said. "I don't know what your purpose is in coming to me, Mrs. Cool, but I'm very much afraid that you're trying to do something that isn't for my best interests. As far as I'm concerned, I'm perfectly satisfied with the situation the way it is."

"But you don't want to take money from an insurance company that—"

"But, Mrs. Cool, just now you were arguing that the insurance company was rolling in money, and that it was quite all right to keep their money."

"Well, that's what *I'd* do under the circumstances," Bertha said. "Of course, if you want to be ethical—"

"Then it's exactly what *I* will do under the circumstances."

"But you'll go after this other insurance company?"

Josephine Dell shook her head.

"Please," Bertha pleaded. "Let me handle it for you. I tell you I can get you some money just like that," and Bertha snapped her fingers.

Josephine Dell smiled. "I'm afraid, Mrs. Cool, that you're trying to— Well, I've heard a lot about how insurance companies try to take advantage of people. I was very much surprised to see how nice Mr. Milbran was. I suppose that the main office didn't like the settlement he'd made with you and is trying to get me to repudiate it. Is that it?"

Bertha said wearily, "That isn't it. It's just like I told you. You got the license number wrong."

"But you can't tell me where I made a mistake in it?"

"No."

"Do you know even one figure in the license number?"

"No. I don't know anything about the *man*. I know the insurance company."

"Do you know the name of the man who hit me?"

Bertha said angrily, "I don't know a damn thing about it."

Josephine Dell picked up her book. "I'm sorry, Mrs. Cool, but I don't think I care to discuss the matter any further. Good morning."

"But, look, did you know Myrna Jackson had been impersonating you? Did you know—"

"I'm sorry, Mrs. Cool. I don't want to discuss the matter with you any further. Good morning!"

"But—"

"Good morning, Mrs. Cool."

Chapter Thirty

IT WAS not until Wednesday morning that Bertha Cool returned to her office.

"Where," Elsie Brand asked, "have *you* been?"

Bertha Cool's sun-bronzed face twisted into a grin. She said, "I've been doing the one thing I'm good at."

"What's that?"

"Fishing."

"You mean you were fishing all day yesterday?"

"Yes. I got so damned exasperated I darn near blew up. I decided to hell with it. I was running a blood pressure of about two hundred and eighty. I climbed in my car, drove down to the beach, rented some fishing-tackle and proceeded to enjoy myself. Do you know what happened? It's an uncanny combination of circumstances, a coincidence that wouldn't happen once in ten million times."

"What?" Elsie Brand asked.

"The man who ran into Josephine Dell was drunk. Josephine Dell thought she took his license number. She didn't. She got the wrong license number. She got a couple of figures juggled somewhere, but, as luck would have it, the man whose license number she did get had also been driving his car and he was also drunk, so drunk that he didn't know but what he actually had hit

179

her. Therefore, she's in the position of being able to collect from two insurance companies, only she hasn't sense enough to—"

"You'd better read Donald Lam's letter first, Mrs. Cool," Elsie Brand said.

"Was there a letter from Donald?"

"He dictated it to me."

"To you!" Bertha Cool exclaimed.

"Yes."

"When?"

"Last night."

"Where?"

"Here at the office."

"You mean Donald Lam was *here?*"

"Yes, he got a thirty-six-hour leave of absence, took a plane down here, and dropped in to see us. My, but he looked swell in his uniform, and he's really filling out. He's getting fit, putting on weight, and looks hard as—"

"Why in hell," Bertha exclaimed, "didn't you get in touch with me?"

"I did everything I could, Mrs. Cool. You told me that you were going to Redlands. I told Donald everything that you had told me, and he started out to Redlands after you. I don't think that you had been gone more than half an hour when Donald came in, and evidently he followed right along behind you. Do you want his letter?"

Bertha snatched the envelope out of Elsie Brand's hand, started for her private office, turned, and snapped over her shoulder, "I don't want to be disturbed. No telephone calls. No visitors. No clients. Nothing."

Elsie Brand nodded.

Bertha, once more seething with indignation, ripped off the end of the sealed envelope, plumped herself down in the chair, and started reading the long letter.

Dear Bertha:

I am very sorry I missed you. I have taken a keen interest in the case from the correspondence, and when I unexpectedly received a thirty-six-hour leave, decided to come down and see what could be done. You weren't in the office. Elsie said you had gone to Redlands where you thought Josephine Dell was or had been located. I hired a car and drove to Redlands.

Because of certain peculiar circumstances, I had already come to the conclusion that Josephine Dell might be in an out-of-town hospital. The fact that *two* gifts had been sent to the blind man, one a very tactful gift such as a sympathetic young woman would give to a man in his position with no note accompanying it, and the other a rather tactless gift accompanied by a note, made me think that there might be two Josephine Dells; one the real Josephine Dell, and the other an impostor.

The conversation you had with the manager of the Bluebonnet Apartments should have shown you that the girl you met who was checking out was the one the manager knew as Myrna Jackson. Recall that conversation, remember your visit the night the girl was checking out, and you'll see the whole thing.

It didn't take me long once I had arrived in Redlands to find Josephine Dell in the sanitarium. I arrived about forty minutes after you had left. I told Miss Dell who I was, and found her in a very hostile and suspicious frame of mind, but she was willing to talk and answer questions and let me explain.

I think you made your mistake, if you will pardon my saying so, in being a little too greedy. You kept looking at it from *your* angle. Because *you* were interested in getting a twenty-five-hundred-dollar cut from the insurance company, you kept thinking of the insurance angle; whereas it was manifestly apparent that this was really a very minor issue.

By being sympathetic and tactful, and convincing Miss Dell that I was trying to right a wrong and clear up an injustice, I was able to get her talking. Once she started talking, the whole solution became apparent.

I first convinced myself that Josephine Dell actually had been employed by Harlow Milbers in his lifetime. I asked her about the occasion when she executed the will as a witness, and she remembered it perfectly. She also remembered that the second witness to the will was not Paul Hanberry at all, but was a man by the name of Dawson who, at that time, had a photographic studio adjoining Harlow Milbers's office. The will was not made at the house at all, but was made at the office.

I got Josephine Dell to sign her name for me. The signature did not in the least agree with the signature of Josephine Dell which was appended to the will.

I had already deduced much of this because I took the precaution of looking up the weather on the twenty-fifth of January, 1942—apparently something you neglected doing. Had you done it, you would have found that it was raining steadily on the twenty-fifth of January. Therefore, Paul Hanberry would hardly have been washing a car in the driveway during a pouring rainstorm.

I also questioned Miss Dell as to the symptoms which accompanied Harlow Milbers's death and found very definitely that he did complain of cramps in the calves of his legs. Under the circumstances, the symptoms are so absolutely typical of arsenic poisoning that it would seem possible to make a very convincing diagnosis for the police.

In short, then, Harlow Milbers was poisoned on Friday morning. He died late Friday afternoon. Josephine Dell, returning home, was struck by an automobile, and had a mild concussion. She called a doctor the next morning when she experienced unusual symptoms. The doctor diagnosed a concussion and suggested she should keep absolutely quiet, preferably that she should go at once to a hospital or a sanitarium. Miss Dell had no money, but she thought that Nettie Cranning might make an advance from the household allowance. She thereupon went to Milbers's residence and explained the circumstances to Nettie Cranning.

That is where Mrs. Cranning showed unusual genius. In place of telephoning to the person who had struck Josephine Dell, she proceeded to get some money. She got some friend of hers to pose as a man named Milbran who claimed to be representing an insurance company which had no actual existence.

By means of this deception, they were able to get Miss Dell out of town and into a sanitarium where she would be out of circulation for at least two months. That gave them ample opportunity to go to work on the will. As I suspected, the first page of the will was genuine. The second page was a complete forgery. You will remember that Myrna Jackson had moved in with Josephine Dell about three weeks prior to the accident. At the time there was no sinister purpose in this whatever. However, it is well to remember that Myrna Jackson was a friend of Mrs. Cranning and of her daughter, Eva, of about the same mental and moral caliber.

Following the death of Harlow Milbers, Nettie Cranning discovered the will. She found that the cousin was cut off with ten thousand dollars. In fact, the first page of that will is absolutely genuine. It wasn't until the next day the possibility of changing the will occurred to Mrs. Cranning, Eva Hanberry, and Paul Hanberry. Mrs. Cranning evidently was the one who conceived the idea. By getting rid of Josephine Dell for two months, they would be able to substitute a second page of the will, leaving most of the property to themselves. You will remember that I pointed out to you the possibility of this in my telegram. It was only necessary to get someone to take the part of Josephine Dell, get her to sign as a witness on the fraudulent second page of the will, have Paul Hanberry also sign as a witness, forge the signature of Harlow Milbers, and then make some compromise with Christopher Milbers, who was the only other relative, get rid of him, and be sitting pretty. The real Josephine Dell was out of circulation for sixty days. The 'insurance company' had promised her a job when she was able to leave the sanitarium. Doubtless that job would have been one which took her to South America or some place where she would never see or hear of Milbers again.

The only fly in the ointment was that the man who

183

had actually hit Josephine Dell and who was intoxicated enough to become obnoxious, was not so intoxicated but what he remembered what had happened after he sobered up. Therefore, he got in touch with his insurance company in a contrite frame of mind, and the insurance company went dashing around trying to square the thing. The accident wasn't reported to the authorities because the driver of the car was so intoxicated the insurance carrier was afraid to let him report the true facts, including the significant fact that he couldn't remember the name of the person whom he had knocked down, etc. etc.

When they saw your ad in the paper asking for a witness, they immediately started work on you, using you as their only possible contact with the person who had been injured. But subsequently Jerry Bollman moved in and doubtless would have chiseled you out in the making of a settlement had it not been that the spurious Josephine Dell was afraid to make a settlement with the insurance company, because she was afraid that, at some time during the negotiations, she would have to meet the driver of the car, who would then brand her as an impostor, and thereby ruin the whole scheme.

One of the most significant clues in the entire matter was that Josephine Dell didn't go near the blind man after she had 'recovered.' This was a bit of rudeness which bothered the blind man very much indeed. Your friend, Jerry Bollman, started pumping the blind man. He began to smell a very large and odoriferous rat, and was shrewd enough to put two and two together. Prior to that time, he had been given a very good inkling of what was going on. Remember that he had telephoned the residence of Harlow Milbers and asked if Josephine Dell was working there. You will also remember that he made this call as a total stranger to her. That is very significant because no one was permitted to contact the person who was posing as Josephine Dell who knew her; but when Bollman said he was a stranger to her, he was given an opportunity to meet her. As soon as he did, he knew that she wasn't the young woman he had seen knocked over; and with a man of Bollman's temperament, that was all that was necessary to put him off on a hot trail.

What he had found out from the fictitious Josephine Dell and what he was able to worm out of the blind man convinced him of the general nature of the conspiracy. He didn't go to the blind man's house in order to get any evidence. He went there for one purpose, *to rig up a snare gun which would kill the blind man*—because, you see, the blind man was the only other possible witness who could upset the deal. Once this snare gun had been set up, so that Kosling would blunder into it and be killed, everything was all set to enjoy the huge estate. A settlement had already been made with Christopher Milbers who would return to Vermont. (Jerry Bollman, of course, was cutting himself in on the whole deal. That was the masterly part of his trap gun. He would leave the blind man in San Bernardino, go to his house, fix up a snare gun, then go to Nettie Cranning, Eva Hanberry, and Paul Hanberry, and declare himself in on the deal. Remember that there were several hundred thousand dollars involved, and Jerry Bollman was a type who valued money above all else.)

If they refused, he would have the blind man as a witness. If they cut him in, he would show them how he had arranged to get rid of the blind man—because, you see, this blind man had all the elements of the truth. He was going to investigate. He thought Josephine had lost her memory. By the time he'd done a little more thinking, he'd have realized the difference in voices. He'd have made trouble. He had started to confide to Thinwell. He was going to get a doctor and confide in him. It was better for all concerned to have Kosling out of the way, if they wanted to be absolutely safe.

The police made the mistake of thinking that the trap gun had been rigged up *by* a blind man since there was no attempt whatever to conceal it. The police overlooked the fact that the trap gun was rigged up *for* a blind man and, therefore, there was no necessity of concealing it.

We can only guess what happened when Jerry Bollman met his death, but, in view of your letters and the report you made to Elsie Brand, I think it is quite apparent. Bollman had rigged up the gun, had everything so arranged that the minute any pressure was brought to bear on the fine wire which crossed the door, the gun would be discharged. He then started out. At that time, the tame bat came flying in out of the darkness, and lit on Bollman's shoulder or fluttered against his face. As was only natural, Bollman jumped back, forgetting for the moment the snare gun. What happened was a masterpiece of poetic justice. He jumped right into the wire.

I think this just about covers the case except that I think you will find there is a very strong possibility Josephine Dell was remembered in the genuine will in a very substantial manner. If the last pages of the will have been destroyed, the contents can still be proved by parol evidence, and it is almost certain that out of Nettie Cranning, Eva Hanberry, and Paul Hanberry, at least one will turn state's evidence in order to get a lighter sentence.

Sergeant Sellers was all wet in fixing the time the trap gun was set as being around three in the afternoon, because the bat was flying around, and bats only fly at night unless they've been disturbed. The shades were all drawn, which made the house pretty dark. Bats fly at dusk. Sergeant Sellers should have known this. Because he didn't, he got his time element all wrong.

Oh, yes, in regard to the death of Harlow Milbers. It is quite obvious that since Nettie Cranning couldn't have foreseen the accident to Josephine Dell which took place *after* that death, they would hardly have planned to kill Harlow Milbers, since, in the ordinary course of things, they could not have substituted the last pages of the will. Questioning Miss Dell, I found that Harlow Milbers was quite fond of genuine maple sugar, that his cousin occasionally sent him bits of maple sugar from his Vermont farm, that on the morning in question, a small package of maple sugar had been received in the mail, and Harlow Milbers had eaten most of it. But there was still a small piece left in his desk drawer. I feel quite certain that an anlysis of this piece will show that Christopher Milbers had attempted to realize on an inheritance by speeding the demise of his crotchety cousin.

Because you weren't available, I turned the facts over to Sergeant Sellers, giving him an opportunity to solve two murder mysteries so that there would be quite a feather in his cap. To say that the sergeant was elated was putting it mildly.

And, oh, yes, I almost forgot. Josephine Dell was very grateful indeed. She executed a power of attorney to the firm, giving us half of whatever we are able to get from the insurance company, and also agreeing to pay us ten per cent of any amounts which she might receive under the will of Harlow Milbers in the event we are able to prove the real contents of that will.

I think this covers everything. You will find the assignments enclosed herewith in due form. I have drawn them myself so as to make certain of their legality. No one seems to know just where you are. I am going to wait until the last possible minute before taking a plane back to San Francisco. It is necessary that I be at the Mare Island Navy Yard promptly on time. You understand that we are at war, and that discipline must be maintained. While I can't mention it publicly and have nothing official to go on, I have reason to believe we are about to start out on what will doubtless prove a very unwelcome little surprise party for our enemies.

I am indeed sorry I missed seeing you, but Elsie will type this out, and I think you will find that you can count on the co-operation of Sergeant Sellers.

Bertha Cool laid the letter down on the desk, fished in the envelope, and brought out the assignments duly executed by Josephine Dell and witnessed by two nurses in the sanitarium.

"Fry me for an oyster," Bertha Cool said.

She reached for a cigarette, but her trembling hands fumbled with the lid of the office humidor.

Bertha heard a commotion in the outer office; then the door burst open. She heard Sergeant Sellers's booming voice saying, "Nonsense, Elsie. Of course, she'll see me. My God, after what she's done for me, I feel like a partner in the firm."

Sergeant Sellers stood in the doorway, a vast hulk of beaming amiability.

"Bertha," he said, "I want to apologize to you. I got a little rough with you, and then, by God, you make me feel like a heel. You heap coals of fire on my head. You give me a chance to crack the two biggest murder cases of my entire career, and you and that nervy little partner of yours step aside so that *I* can take the credit. I just want to shake hands with you."

Sergeant Sellers came barging across the office, his hand outstretched.

Bertha got to her feet, gripped Sergeant Sellers's hand. "Things work out all right?" she asked.

"Just exactly as you and Donald blocked them out for me. Bertha, if there's ever anything you want from the police department, anything that I can do for you, all you've got to do is to say so. I think you understand that. I—I—dammit, come here."

Sergeant Sellers threw a big arm around Bertha Cool's massive shoulders, tilted her chin with his big hamlike hand, and kissed her on the mouth.

"There," he said, releasing her. *"That's* the way I feel."

Bertha Cool dropped weakly into a chair.

"Can me for a sardine," she said weakly. "I'm just a poor fish."

>>> If you've enjoyed this book and would like to discover more great vintage crime and thriller titles, as well as the most exciting crime and thriller authors writing today, visit: >>>

The Murder Room
Where Criminal Minds Meet

themurderroom.com